An Intrepid Mountie

Adventures of the First

Woman Mountie. Book 8

LAURIE SCHRAMM

This book is a work of historical fiction, set in the 1970s. Although most of the historical references are accurate, a few are not, and names, characters, places, and incidents are either the product of the author's imagination or are used fictitiously. Any resemblance to actual persons, living or dead is entirely coincidental.

Print ISBN: 978-1-7772424-6-6
ePub ISBN: 978-1-7772424-7-3

Laurie Schramm

DEDICATION

To Staff Sergeant Al Lund (RCMP, Ret.), author
of *Mounties on the Cover* and probably the
world's leading authority on Mountie fiction.

Laurie Schramm

CONTENTS

Laurie Schramm

ACKNOWLEDGMENTS

I am extremely grateful to the growing number of friendly readers that that have provided encouragement, comments, and suggestions based on drafts of these books: Ann Marie, Victoria, Katherine, William, Al, Dawson, Jayme, Moira, Karen, and Ernie.

Special thanks also to three real-life veterans of the RCMP, all of whom have supplemented their encouragement with numerous background and factual reference materials on the Force: Chief Superintendent William Schramm (Ret.), who also kindly allowed my main character to borrow his Regimental Number, Assistant Commissioner Dawson Hovey (Ret.), and Staff Sergeant Al Lund (Ret., author of *Mounties on the Cover* and probably the world's leading authority on Mountie fiction).

Laurie Schramm

LIST OF CHARACTERS
(IN ORDER OF APPEARANCE)

- Major David Jones, U.S. Army Special Forces
- Michael (Mickey) Webb, Captain of the *MV Ocean Saviour*
- Corporal Alexandra (Alex) Houston, RCMP
- Silver, an Alaskan Malamute. Alex's friend and partner
- Arne Kristiansen, President, International Alliance for Animal Protection (IAAP)
- Staff Sergeant Robert (Bob) G. Simpson, RCMP
- Special Agent Vivian Rule, FBI
- Ginger Brandt, Canadian TV and film actress
- Sam Hynes, a sailor on the *MV Ocean Saviour*
- George O'Dell, tour boat operator, Bay Bulls, NF
- Jimmy O'Dell, George's son
- Lieutenant Commander Jon Stanford, Captain of the *CCGS John A. Macdonald*.
- Sergeant Al Donaldson, RCMP, St. Anthony Detachment
- Constable Nick Ross, RCMP, St. Anthony Detachment
- James MacDonald, a young fisherman from St. John's, NF

CIDG Strike Force Patch

1 FIRST PRELUDE: THE MAJOR

January 2, 1964
Buon Enao,
A small village in South Vietnam's Central Highlands.

Although it was the day after New Year's Day, it was still hot at 90°F. At least it was the dry season. As the sun settled into dusk, the relative silence of the jungle was broken by the sound of an approaching helicopter. The sound became louder and louder as it appeared over the top of the surrounding jungle. Visible now, it was an older model 'Huey.'

The first Hueys were properly named Bell UH-1 Iroquois, and had been used extensively by the American military in Vietnam since 1960. The nickname "Huey" came from the original designation as HU-1. Despite its redesignation (in 1962) to UH-1, the nickname had stuck. This particular Huey was fitted out as a 'Cobra,' that is, a gunship. Both of the large sliding doors were latched open and onto each side had been bolted a swivel-mount (called a pintle) bearing an M60 7.62mm machine gun. The U.S. Army had deployed thousands of Hueys during the Vietnam War, so they were a common sight.

This particular Huey bore the common U.S. Army olive drab, except for the nose, which was covered with a flat-black antiglare paint. The paint on this particular Huey was well faded, and it carried no identifying markings. It was, however, expected.

Close to the village of Buon Enao was a fortified camp of the U.S. Army Special Forces. It was laid out in the shape of a square, with a defensive berm around the entire circumference and twin .30 calibre machine guns placed at each corner and halfway along each side. Inside the camp were barracks and other buildings, most of them occupied by members of the Civilian Irregular Defense Group[1] (CIDG). Although the camp was commanded by a Vietnamese Special Forces Commander, it was a U.S. Special Forces Captain - the local military 'advisor' - that was waiting at a clearing just outside the fortified berm.

Having circled the camp and seen nothing of concern, the helicopter descended diagonally towards the clearing and landed. As the rotor blades slowed, the waiting captain could see that the machine gun positions at each door were unmanned, and that the Cobra carried only a single pilot. As the main rotor slowed to a lazy crawl, the pilot climbed down from the left-hand pilot's door and walked across the clearing. The pilot wore a green beret and was dressed in a U.S. Army Special Forces uniform that bore a major's golden oak leaves but no unit patches. "Captain?" he said, extending a hand when he was close enough.

"Yes. Major Jones, I presume." The two men shook hands. It was clear that Jones was not the pilot's real name.

"You have the Deer Guns?" asked the pilot.

"Right here," said the captain, pointing to three medium-size wooden crates. When they'd walked over, he lifted the lid from one of the crates. Inside were packed styrofoam boxes, each containing a small, clumsy-looking pistol, three cartridges, and a cartoon-picture sheet of instructions on how to load and fire the gun.

As both men knew, the Deer Guns were disposable CIA assassination pistols[2], designed to be provided to South Vietnamese guerrillas - such as the CIDG — for use against North Vietnamese soldiers. The idea was that they would kill the enemy soldiers, dispose of the pistol, and arm themselves with the victim's more powerful (and expensive) arms and other equipment.

"This is all of them?" asked the pilot.

"Yes, 150 of them were shipped here last year for field testing but by the time they arrived we were already providing the Yards[3] with much better weapons, so these were never used. This is all of them. Seems like a shame to destroy them all, but the directive from MACV[4] was very

clear...." He paused, then said "You know I'm going to need some kind of receipt, right?"

"No problem," said the pilot, taking a folded piece of paper from his pocket. The paper was actually a three-sheet form with carbon paper between each form. It had already been filled in for materiel disposal, specifying the type and quantity of pistols. Taking out a ballpoint pen, the pilot signed the form as Major Davy Jones, U.S. Army Special Forces.

"Davy Jones?" said the captain with a smirk.

"It's as good a name as any, and this form will cover your ass."

"Sounds good to me. Do you want one of the copies?"

The pilot snorted. "Not likely, I'd just have to burn it. If you'll give me a hand with these crates, I'll give you your reward."

It only took a few minutes to carry the three 60-pound crates to the helicopter and stow them at the rear of the cabin. Then the pilot opened the right-hand door and extracted three large bottles of French Brandy.

"Here you are. One bottle for each crate, as agreed."

"Thank you major," said the captain, cradling the bottles under one arm. "I assume you're not really going to destroy the guns?"

The pilot just looked at him for a moment; long enough for the captain to decide that he wasn't going to get an answer. But he did.

"I'll tell you this much. These guns will never be seen in Vietnam again."

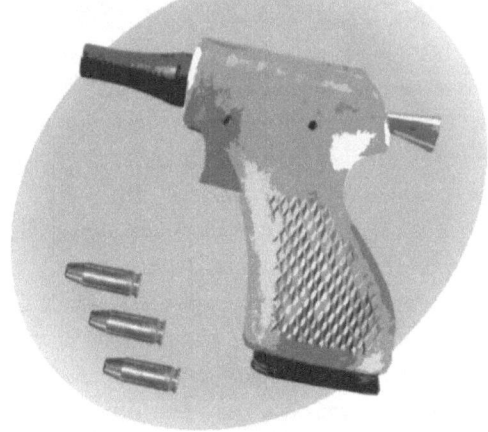

CIA Deer Gun (1962-64)

May 3, 1970
Kent State University
Kent, Ohio, U.S.A.

A shadowy figure joined the hundreds of students and other protesters as they gathered for a second day of protests against the escalation of the Vietnam War.

Although the President had promised to end the war, in seeming contradiction, just two days earlier he had sent U.S. troops to invade Cambodia, from which North Vietnamese troops had been launching attacks on the South. The very next day, hundreds of students had gathered on the university's Commons to speak out against the war. With the onset of night, peaceful assembly and speeches had been marred by incidents of violence between protesters and police. The mayor's decision to close the city's bars infuriated additional people, and the size and spread of the crowd increased. Eventually, the police resorted to using tear gas to break up the crowds.

Now, on day two, a state of emergency had been declared and the Ohio National Guard was reportedly on its way. Nevertheless, hundreds of students and other protesters had once again descended on the university campus. As evening approached, tempers again frayed and skirmishes began to erupt. The shadowy figure had thick, long hair, wore aviator-style sunglasses, and was dressed to fit in with the crowd, with a tie-dyed t-shirt sporting a carved wooden peace symbol, faded jeans and dirty sneakers. As such, he bore little resemblance to the U.S. Special Forces persona that he had adopted while working in South Vietnam.

As he wove his way through the crowd his senses were alert to the emotions around him. He was searching for a cluster of people that might be angry enough to cause some real trouble.

Like all major U.S. campuses, Kent State had a Reserve Officers' Training Corps (ROTC) building, and it was there that he found what he was looking for. A large cluster of protesters near the building were yelling, screaming, and throwing rocks and beer bottles at the police. As he skirted around this cluster, he could see that the police, for their part, were preparing to respond with tear gas. The time is just about right, *he thought.*

Moving even further to one side, he was able to make his way around the crowd and around the building. Although the back doors were locked, he had no trouble using a knife to force open one of the large, multipaned ground-floor windows and enter the building. Being a Saturday evening, the interior of the building was deserted and he was able to quickly roam the hallways peering into each room until he found what he was looking for. One of the large rooms had clearly been dedicated to assembling and storing promotional pamphlets for the ROTC Program. Various pamphlets were piled on large work tables, along with portfolio covers into which they would be inserted, and in two corners of the room were piled boxes of heavyweight paper waiting to be printed. As luck would have it, this room had windows that faced out of the front of the building. Perfect, *he thought.*

Moving to one of the piles of boxes, he cut one open and began removing handfuls of paper, which he tore into strips and used to make a large pile. Then, striding to the nearest table he picked up one of the wooden chairs, raised it high over his head and brought it down with a crash onto the edge of the table. The table was strong, having been made of thick oak, whereas the chair was old enough that the dowels holding it together had long lost most of their integrity. The chair splintered into pieces. Gathering up the pieces, he used them to make a teepee-shape over his pile of shredded paper. From his back pocket he took a hip flask of the kind that was popularly used to carry bourbon. It was full, but not with bourbon. The flask contained 'white gas' camp fuel.

Emptying the entire flask onto the pile of shredded paper, he took out a box of wooden matches, lighted one and gently tossed it to the edge of the pile, then quickly stepped back. Almost instantaneously there was a loud "whoosh" sound and a blaze of intense flame. Without waiting for the wood to ignite, which would happen momentarily, he walked calmly back down the hallways, pausing only to step into the men's restroom, where he used soap, water, and paper towel to remove any fingerprints from the hip flask and then threw everything into the trash.

By the time he had exited the building and made his way around the edge of the crowd, which was still protesting in front of the building, he could see through two of the front windows a reddish glow that evidenced a growing fire.

He waited a few moments, for the glow to increase, then yelled out: "Look, someone's burning down the ROTC. Let's help them."

Almost immediately, the crowd surged and he could hear the crashing sounds of bottles and rocks being thrown through the ROTC Building's windows. This, of course, caused an inrush of fresh air that fanned the flames, which almost immediately engulfed much of the ground floor room in which the fire had been originally been set.

By the time the National Guard arrived, later that evening, the university's ROTC Building was fully ablaze, the police were again using tear gas in an attempt to break up the crowds but, undeterred, the cheering from hundreds of protesters drowned out even the sounds of the sirens from the approaching fire trucks.

By this time, the silent figure was long gone. As he calmly strode across the campus, he removed his peace sign and dropped it into a trash can, disposed of his sunglasses at another trash can, and then removed and discarded his wig just before leaving the campus altogether, for the moment.

Despite the presence of the National Guard and officers from several police forces, and notwithstanding the efforts of the university to ban further mass gatherings, several thousand people turned up at the

Commons the next morning. As the crowd gathered, the same shadowy figure from the previous day joined in. Had anyone looked closely, it would have been difficult to identify him as such, as he now wore a differently coloured and styled wig, John Lennon-style sunglasses, an open-neck Hawaiian-style shirt, and a necklace bearing a peace medallion.

As various people took turns making brief speeches through a megaphone, the Ohio National Guard attempted to halt the speeches. This was met with derision, anger, and rock throwing. After a brief interlude, the national guard attempted to disperse the crowd. This time, rock throwing was met with tear gas, which was ineffective due to wind. The guards next tried fixing bayonets on the rifles and advancing towards the crowd. This was somewhat effective in moving the crowd back, but as the crowd retreated the advancing guards, for some reason, took a slightly different route and found themselves blocked by a large fence. As the protesters kept moving around, the guards decide they had achieved their purpose in clearing the Commons and began to make their way back. As they did so, large groups of the protesters followed them, still throwing rocks and tear gas canisters.

With the protesters now advancing, and the guardsmen looking nervous, the figure in the Hawaiian shirt moved near the front of the crowd, took out a small pistol that had been tucked into his waistband, and fired at a sergeant, grazing the side of one leg[5]. In response, the sergeant began firing his pistol into the crowd, followed by nearly thirty other guardsmen who immediately shouldered and fired their rifles at the students.

By this time, the figure in the Hawaiian shirt had already faded to the back. Just before leaving the crowd he used his shirt to wipe any fingerprints off of the gun, then simply dropped it on the ground and walked out of the crowd and away. When he passed Taylor Hall, he turned left, walking between it and Prentice Hall. Between the two buildings, largely screened from most people's sight, he removed his wig, peace-medallion necklace, and sunglasses. Next, he did the same with his Hawaiian Shirt, revealing a simple but differently coloured t-shirt. The Hawaiian Shirt he carried crumpled up in one hand.

Emerging from between the two buildings and calmly striding across the campus, he dropped the necklace and sunglasses into a trash can, then the wig into another trash can. The Hawaiian Shirt, he discarded at yet another trash as he continued to walk back towards the Commons.

The man was satisfied with his performance. He had judged the timing perfectly and baited the national guard into firing indiscriminately into the crowd. There were bound to have been at least a few casualties. The point was to create an event that would horrify America and catalyze angry, possibly violent protests across the country.

He succeeded. The guards' bullets had struck 13 students, three of whom were shot in the back, and four of whom died. The shootings at Kent State led to protests and strikes at universities across the United States, not to mention a protest demonstration by a hundred thousand people in Washington, D.C., itself - fuelled by chants like "Four Dead in Ohio[6]" and "They Can't Kill Us All."

His masters' hopes of bringing an early end to the war, however, failed. Notwithstanding the massive and wide-ranging protests that were precipitated by the Kent State events, the war continued for several more years[7].

In the aftermath of the four days of demonstrations, the FBI discovered a small, single-shot pistol lying on the university grounds where the students had made their last stand. A few members of the FBI had heard rumours of such guns being made for the CIA, this was the first physical example they'd actually encountered.

It would not be the last....

2 SECOND PRELUDE: THE ACTIVISTS

"Before the turn of the century... riots were spontaneous and practically leaderless. They were not the offspring of sobering thought or calculating mind, but were the sudden outbursts of passion. The leaders of these mobs were characterized as the most angry and least discreet members of the mob. [Later], though, a change in the nature of the mob took place... [and] professional agitators were part and parcel of [these events]8."

March, 1978
'The Front,'
100 miles southeast of Labrador

Captain Michael (Mickey) Webb stood on the bridge with his feet slightly spread out for stability. An experienced sailor, this was all he needed to do to maintain his balance, so he was easily able to use both hands to hold and focus the binoculars through which he was peering ahead in the dawn's first light.

The water is certainly choppy enough, *he thought,* as the MV Ocean Saviour *relentlessly pushed its way towards the icepack off the coast of Labrador. Although stable in the water it was not a gentle ride, particularly since the originally fitted external stabilizers had been removed. In fact, when the former marine meteorological and oceanographic research ship had been purchased by the Ocean Saviour Foundation, a number of ice-strengthening modifications had been made. To the pre-existing double hull, an ice belt had been added – a very thick layer of structurally supported steel at the lower part of the bow. This and the double hull were intended to provide a buffer in case of a collision with ice (or another ship).*

This was not to say that the ship was an icebreaker, but rather that it was capable of Arctic or Antarctic operations "where ice regimes permit," as the ship's certification papers read. This official language meant that it was fully capable of ramming its way through seasonal and even Second-Year Ice, but not the much heavier Multi-Year Ice. As it was, the modifications had cost upwards of a million dollars, not considering the original purchase price.

The ship itself was the flagship of the Ocean Saviour Foundation. Not that this designation meant a lot, considering that the rest of the 'fleet' consisted of small Zodiac™ boats, but it was a recognizable symbol of the society and its cause and its supporters hoped it would be the first of many such ships. The 500 gross-ton ship measured 184 ft (56 m) in length, was classed as a Research/Survey Vessel, carried a crew complement of up to 35 and was capable of 18 knots (33 km/h).

The Ocean Saviour travelled the world. Their most recent voyages had been to the waters between California and Hawaii, where they had harassed Russian whaling ships with such tactics[9] as using Zodiac[10] boats to prevent the whalers from firing their harpoon cannons, getting close enough to obtain graphic film recordings of the whale killings, especially those of undersized whales, and even boarding some whaling ships to distribute anti-whaling materials to the crews.

Now on the opposite side of the continent, their current mission was to interrupt the annual commercial seal hunt off Canada's East Coast. Such hunts occur in two main areas: one in 'the Gulf' meaning the southern Gulf of St. Lawrence (between Newfoundland and the Magdalen Islands), and the other in "the Front" meaning the area southeast of Labrador and northeast of Newfoundland. Right now, they were at the Front, where about half a million seals were reportedly gathered on 60 square miles (155 km²) of pack ice. Here, when the pack ice was available, the female harp seals had gathered to give birth and nurse their pups.

"There they are," said Captain Webb to the helmsman. "Come right, 10 degrees. Half ahead."

Before long, the seals were visible to the naked eye, and the captain called out "Slow ahead. Prepare to strike the ice."

That last command caused a flurry of action as the warning was broadcast throughout the entire ship and crew members scurried around making preparations.

Meanwhile, the slowing ship continued its approach.

After about five minutes of this, the captain decided they had more than enough momentum and ordered "Slow astern."

As the single propeller stopped and then began thrashing the water in reverse, the ship's bow struck and was driven well up onto a huge ice floe carrying a large number of seals. At this point, rope ladders were dropped from each side of the bow and a dozen young men and women scrambled down and onto the ice. Each of them had strapped to their back a portable sprayer of the type commonly used for spraying weeds in a lawn or garden. As they approached, the seals continued to lie on the ice, taking at best only a cursory interest in the newcomers.

Each protester slipped the sprayer off their back, placed the tank vertically on the ice, and pressurized it by hand-pumping. Grasping the spray wand with one hand, the other was used to twist its nozzle to a desired spray pattern. Then, using one hand to lift and carry the tank and the other hand to aim the spray, they stepped around the seals, searching out the 'whitecoats.' These were six- to twelve-day old harp seal pups, highly prized for their pure-white fur. Each whitecoat was sprayed with the contents of the tank: a nontoxic green dye. When the tank pressure fell off, the protester would stop, pump the pressure back up, and continue spraying.

The idea was that the brightly-coloured, indelible dye would eliminate the commercial value of the whitecoats' fur, thereby saving them from death at the hands of the sealers. Accompanying the protesters were several reporters and photographers from CBC, NBC, The New York Times, *and* Der Stern. *These were busily filming and photographing the event. It was because of the media that green dye had been chosen. In earlier protests, red dye had been used, but the resulting photographs didn't look sufficiently different from photographs of bloody pups being killed by the sealers, hence the change to green.*

Before long, the sounds of five short blasts from the ship's horn were heard. This is a nautical signal for danger, in this case meaning that the whaling ships — and probably police — were approaching. By this time many hundreds of pups had been sprayed, so everyone quite contentedly stopped what they were doing and made their way back to the ship. When everyone was back aboard, the captain ordered "Full astern," and the ship backed off the ice.

As the sealers continued to approach the ice pack, the Ocean Saviour *moved diagonally away and accelerated to full speed, heading for port. Captain Mickey Webb was well satisfied. They had saved hundreds of baby seals and, more importantly, should receive a wave of useful publicity when the media stories, photos, and documentary footage were broadcast by the media. One of the reporters had already been overheard planning to do a feature 'David and Goliath' type story on the youthful idealists taking on the grizzled, money-grubbing sealers. He didn't expect much in the way of retaliation. Beyond revoking permits, there was little that the Canadian government could do to them.*

A Saturday in March, 1978
Toronto, Ontario

The demonstration's beginning was orderly enough. Several hundred people, mostly women, had gathered in front of the two curved towers that housed City Hall – one of Toronto's most famous landmarks. The women were there to show their support for women's rights[11], and to hear from various speakers on the topic.

Some of the speeches were broad in nature. One speaker, for example, railed against the nonsensical idea that women could (and should) find fulfillment only through childrearing and homemaking. "It's 1978," the speaker called out. "We shouldn't have to still be having this conversation in this day and age."

Other speeches were more focused. One of the speakers related the plight of women workers at a Southern Ontario manufacturing plant, in which working conditions had become so bad that they had just staged a walkout in protest[12] and were still out on strike. The speaker listed the women's working conditions, which included operating dangerous equipment, virtually intolerable heat (in the summer), cold (in the winter), and harassment from male supervisors, all for less pay than male maintenance workers in the same plant, no benefits, and no job security.

As the speeches progressed, the size of the crowd grew. Mostly they were women but there was a sizeable number of men as well. They came from all kinds of backgrounds and circumstances. There were university and college students, of course, but also office workers, factory workers, part-time workers, and others.

Woven into the speeches were attempts to rally the people in attendance with calls to action. Meanwhile, volunteers circulated through the crowd handing out placards to carry and wave. The placards carried slogans like **"Yes It's Time,"** and **"Equity – Now!"**

Following the speeches, one of the organizers explained that their main objective was to achieve gender equity in Ontario's Labour Laws, so it was provincial politicians that needed convincing. Accordingly, everyone was asked to march – in solidarity – to the Provincial Legislature and let their voices be heard.

By this time the crowd was sufficiently roused that they

marched *en masse*, chanting and waving their placards as they marched from City Hall to University Ave. Once there, they spilled out over the sidewalk to fill the entirety of the two northbound lanes leading to Queen's Park (about 25 minutes away).

As news of the march spread, more people joined and what had started as a few hundred became a few thousand. One of the later additions to the crowd was a grey-haired, rather matronly-appearing woman complete with granny-style glasses, full-length skirt, and even a shawl. Although one could have been forgiven for assuming her to be someone's grandmother, a careful observer would have noticed that she seemed remarkably nimble, and that she was able to navigate within the moving crowd with surprising ease.

When the demonstrators reached the south lawn of the Ontario Legislature, they stopped. This was their ultimate destination. It was also where they met a large police presence: the riot squad and 200 additional police officers.

At first, the crowd contented themselves with chanting and waving their placards. For a moment, there was a feeling of optimism as the Minister for Labour came out to address the crowd with a bullhorn. As the Minister spoke, it quickly became clear that he was unacquainted with the issues, spoke in condescending platitudes, and asked everyone to quietly go home where they belonged.

If he expected meek compliance, he had greatly underestimated the demonstrators who immediately became angry again, some of whom began lobbing rocks and beer cans over the front wall of riot shields and into the deeper layers of police officers. At this, some of the police officers visibly began preparations to return fire with tear gas canisters.

Near, but not quite at the front of the line of demonstrators the grey-haired woman judged that the time for escalation was just about right. Reaching into her oversized purse, which resembled a messenger bag in size and shape, she withdrew a glass beer-bottle that had a wick extending beyond a tightly fitted cork stopper. Using a powerful underhand throw, she unobtrusively lobbed it into the back ranks of the police cordon.

Even to the people standing near her, it appeared that she was simply throwing a beer bottle. This was because it wasn't an ordinary Molotov Cocktail, and she hadn't had to light the wick before throwing it. Inside the bottle, besides the fuel mixture of gasoline and motor oil, had been placed a certain amount of concentrated sulfuric acid. The wick, for its part, had been treated with a mixture of crystallized potassium chlorate and sugar. These features made the fuel self-igniting[13] once the bottle was broken.

Indeed, when the bottle smashed on the concrete roadway near the back of the police ranks, there was an immediate burst of purple-tinged flame followed by a cloud of smoke and burning droplets of fuel that spread out in all directions.

Several of the police officers already had their gas masks on and immediately sent four canisters of tear gas flying out and into the middle of the crowd of protesters.

By this time, the woman had already slithered to a new position near, but not quite at, the front of the demonstrators. Reaching into her purse, she withdrew another beer-bottle and again used an underhand throw to lob it into the ranks of the police cordon. When the bottle smashed on the ground, another burst of purple-tinged flame erupted spraying burning fuel in all directions, accompanied by another cloud of smoke. Here again, several nearby police officers responded by tossing tear gas canisters into the crowd which, predictably, triggered more rock and bottle throwing by the demonstrators.

The grey-haired woman, who had already taken up a third position near the front of the protestors reached once again into her bag and this time withdrew a small, ugly-looking pistol. Aiming from the hip and being careful to maintain a line-of-sight between the protestors that were immediately in front of her, she shot into the police ranks.

"They're shooting at us!" she yelled, in as a high-pitched voice as she could.

This caused some people to hurl more debris, including some of the landed tear gas canisters, into the police ranks, while others tried to stampede in virtually every direction only to find themselves running into other people.

The police incident commander had the presence of mind to yell "Hold Your Fire!" and almost all of the officers were able to hear and respond to this command – barely – although another volley of tear gas cannisters was fired into the crowd and a couple of officers discharged their firearms without really aiming at anything.

As confusion, smoke and tear gas swelled in both the police and demonstrators' ranks, the grey-haired woman nimbly slipped diagonally to the back and one side of the crowd. As soon as she reached the edge of the crowd, however, she slowed to a pace more befitting of an elderly woman, adopted a slightly hunched walking style, and calmly walked across the grounds and onto University Avenue heading south, back towards City Hall.

Somewhat before reaching Queen Street, she turned left and proceeded between the courthouse and Osgoode Hall, then past the fountain at Nathan Phillips Square, and finally entered the City Hall Branch of the Toronto Public Library. Strolling through the library she found an unoccupied, well-screened corner between the tall rows of shelving, and turned the now-empty purse inside out so that it now clearly appeared to be what it really was – a common messenger-style shoulder bag. Looking around to make sure she was unobserved, she removed her granny-style glasses, grey wig, and shawl, all of which went into the bag. The back of her floor-length dress had a continuous seam secured with Velcro strips, so that it was only the work of a moment to pull it open from each side and slip out of the sleeves. This too went into the bag.

Now fully revealed for what he really was, a middle-aged man, he walked to the men's washroom, where he washed off the makeup he had been wearing to smooth out his cheeks and chin.

Exiting the washroom, and library, he simply walked away. As he did so, it occurred to him to wonder whether the people that had hired him wanted the protesters to win or lose their struggle.... He shrugged his shoulders. It didn't matter.

A *Toronto Star* headline the next day read "Police Fire into Crowd of Mothers and Grandmothers."

3 ANOTHER PROTEST MOVEMENT

"The better part of valour is discretion; in the which better part I have saved my life."

Sir John Falstaff, In *Henry IV, Part One*, Act V, Scene 4, W. Shakespeare, 1597

July 9, 1978
Ottawa, Ontario

The street was crowded as I turned onto Wellington Street, heading east.

Very crowded for a Sunday! I thought.

The people were mostly young – in their twenties for the most part. There were also quite a few older teenagers, of the 16 to 19 sort and there were also some upper-middle-aged people – in their 40s and 50s. It was the people that weren't there that caught my attention.

What I didn't see many of, were families with small children, people in their early teens, people in their thirties, or seniors – or tourists, even. This struck me as an interesting demographic mix, or absence if you like, for a summer afternoon in Ottawa, the nation's capital. There were some tourists about, of course, but their presence was dwarfed by the others.

The crowd seemed to be heading towards the Parliament Buildings, whose grounds are on the north side of the street, so I stayed on the south side of the street so I could avoid being caught-up in the press of people. That was the other thing about the crowd, they weren't out for a casual afternoon stroll. They were heading somewhere specific, and were moving purposefully enough to suggest that they were on a schedule.

Sure enough, as the people passed the westernmost of the main parliament buildings – named, appropriately enough, the West Block - they turned onto the Parliament Grounds, and dispersed across the broad lawns that lie between the Centennial Flame, which was quite close to the street, and the main Parliament Building, Centre Block, the one with the tall Peace Tower at its front. Although the front lawns were huge, they were about half covered with people, as the crowd I had been paralleling joined an even larger crowd that was already there.

Looking back down the street behind me, there were many more people coming our way as well.

"This is going to be a big one!" I said to Silver, my friend and partner.

Perhaps I should back up a bit and tell you some of my story.

My name is Corporal Alexandra Houston. My friends call me Alex. Four years previously, in the summer of 1974, I'd been 24 years old, and feeling like my career was at a standstill. I'd studied chemistry at university and liked it, but not enough to pursue science as a career. I'd reset my sights on police work next and had joined the Metropolitan Toronto Police force (Metro). Although policing seemed like a better fit for me than science, my two years with Metro had mostly comprised routine administrative- and traffic duties. These assignments were important, and needed to be done by somebody, and done well. But for me, they didn't fit the Hollywood vision of policing that I had developed, and I hadn't found them to be very challenging.

They say you should be careful what you wish for.

At about the same time, Assistant Commissioner George MacLeod of the Royal Canadian Mounted Police (RCMP) had been looking for an existing police officer, with one of Canada's provincial or municipal

18

police forces, for a special pilot project he had in mind. He wanted someone who wanted to accomplish things, someone eager and tenacious, someone chomping at the bit to be allowed to do some 'real' police work, and... someone female. My Captain had recommended the "biggest pain in the butt" in his Division - me.

When we first met, Assistant Commissioner MacLeod explained that the 'Force' wanted to begin engaging women as regular Members. As the RCMP training centre at 'Depot Division' was under his command, this task had been given to him and he wanted to first try a 'pilot test' with a woman. But, he emphasized, that pilot test had to succeed as it would pave the way for an entire first troop of policewomen that would follow. He had thought of using someone that had already qualified as a policewoman, and simply re-train them in the 'RCMP way.'

I had not been enthusiastic about doing basic training all over again, but I did. In the fall of 1974, I went through training at 'Depot' Division in Regina, dealt with the good and the bad issues that came with being the first woman to train there, and survived to become the first woman Mountie. I hadn't intended for it to happen, really. The opportunity just came and found me.

After training, or re-training if you like, I'd been posted to Radium City, a small town in very northern Saskatchewan that, in its early days, had been a great uranium mining centre. Although my new boss, Corporal Morrison, had told me that nothing interesting ever happened around there, he'd been wrong, and I'd had to rescue him from a mine collapse, run our entire detachment single-handed while he was confined to hospital for six weeks, get rescued by a strange dog from near-death, solve a mystery, and find and catch a murderer – all in only four months!

The dog was named Silver. Investigating a mysterious series of break-ins had led me to some unusual places, including several abandoned uranium mines. In one such mine I'd fallen through a trap and found myself hanging precariously over the sharp edge of a vertical mine shaft. Unable to get out and tiring fast, I was saved by the almost magical appearance of what I first took to be a wolf, which gave me quite a scare, but turned out to be Silver, an Alaskan Malamute. Silver somehow sensed that I was in danger, had decided to help, and with his assistance

I had been able to climb up and out of the raise. To make a long story short[14], while I'd continued to investigate the case, he had attached himself to me, was eventually given to me, and we'd been close friends ever since.

Sometime later I'd found myself in another surprise meeting with the same Assistant Commissioner MacLeod. Once again, he had something new in mind for me. By this time, he'd become head of the Force's Security Service[15] and, unsurprisingly, he had some new ideas he wanted to try out by way of some experimental pilot projects. One of them involved me.

That had taken me to Ottawa, where I joined the Security Service. My new boss, Staff Sergeant Robert (Bob) Simpson, introduced me to the shady worlds of spies, counter-espionage, anarchists, and terrorists.

As a prelude to my first real Security Service assignment, Silver and I were sent to Innisfail, Alberta, to be trained as a police dog and handler team[16]. "If that dog is going to go everywhere with you, then we should get him trained too," Assistant Commissioner MacLeod had announced, on one of his periodic visits. Both Bob and the Assistant Commissioner had been interested in the possibilities presented by the first female 'Mountie,' especially undercover possibilities, and they were also interested in, and seemingly amused by, the notion of me having Silver along as a kind of side-kick, since he looked absolutely nothing like a police dog. That officially brought Silver into the Mounties too, and that's how my best friend became my partner.

Since then, we've had more hair-raising adventures together[17-21] and our destinies have been firmly inter-twined.

***

Now, on this sunny Sunday afternoon Silver and I crossed the street at the next intersection. I was wearing civilian clothes, including an Ottawa Rough Riders[22] cap, baggy shorts, lightweight hiking boots, and a small daypack. I was trying to look like a slightly older version of the university student that I once was. A graduate student and/or teaching assistant, perhaps.

Since we weren't in uniform, Silver had to be on a leash - which he tolerated, but not before giving me some pointedly martyred looks from time to time.

Silver's Version

I don't mind the broad leather collar that Alex had made for me not long after we'd first met. I do not, however, like the leash, especially since Alex knows me well enough to know that I never stray far from her without good reason.

There are times, however, when she insists that it is a necessary custom and I trust her judgement, although I always make sure that she understands my feelings in the matter. To be fair, the leash isn't imposed very often.

As we crossed the busy street to where most of the people were gathering, my senses went from being pleasantly distracted to overloaded. There were so many people of different sizes, shapes and expressions, and even more scents.

Some of the people were carrying banners and signs. The signs that humans make are still something of a mystery to me. I have learned a few of their symbols, through experience and constant repetition, but certainly not many. I can understand quite a few words, including most of the things Alex says to me and some of the things that others say to her – if they speak slowly enough – but much of what other people say to each other is a mystery to me unless I can look into their eyes while they are speaking.

I don't know why eye contact is important, but it seems to have something to do with my ability to sense thoughts and feelings. My sister and I became so good at this, as puppies, that we could carry on simple conversations with each other, supplemented and punctuated by the noises we could make with our mouths and throats.

As Alex and I walked into the thick of the crowd, I tried to ignore the sights and smells and focus on my other senses. As I did, it seemed to me that some people were there for a reason. I couldn't tell what they were thinking, but I sensed that there was a purpose to their thoughts. Other people seemed to be almost aimlessly walking about, being carried along with the rest of the crowd without necessarily knowing what it was all about. I even got the clear sense, from the occasional person, that they were actually wondering what it was all about.

We didn't have much trouble mingling with the people in the crowd. I'm not a small dog, and I've heard many people remark on how much they think I look like a large wolf. Although that pleases me, it means that some people are instinctively afraid, or at least wary, of me. As a result, the crowd didn't press against me too much.

Since Alex was able to look ahead better than I could, I was simply walking beside her and following wherever she led until my senses were struck by something new and I stopped to look around in an attempt to identify the source. Alex sensed this immediately and stopped.

"What is it Silver?" she asked. "Smell something?"

I gave a low whine in acknowledgement, as I continued to sweep my head this way and that. Something didn't seem right.

Then, I had it. There was something… that way! I tugged at the leash and led us sharply off to the left. Alex was willing to follow along, and let me lead into a different part of the crowd.

At first, I had to weave back and forth a bit trying to find the source, but eventually the sense I'd picked up became sharper and I could approach it more or less directly. When we were close enough to be able to see the cause, I stopped and stared.

The disconcerting sense I'd picked up had been new and confusing, but now I knew why. There were two overlapping thought patterns, but I could now separate them and identify their sources.

Standing not far away, with their backs to us, were two human males. One quite large, and the other quite average. They were speaking to each other, but in low tones such that I couldn't identify many specific words.

Alex crouched down to one knee, so she could place her head near mine. She had immediately sensed that that the fur was rising on the back of my neck, and I knew that with her hand on my back she could feel the tension in my body.

"Something wrong? Is it those two men?"

"Grrruph," I said, in acknowledgement, but not loudly.

Looking her straight in the eyes, I tried to project the sense of evil I was picking up. Not danger, precisely. Not imminent danger, anyway.

I sensed a dark kind of purposefulness in the thoughts of the larger man. In the 'average' man's mind, I sensed utter blackness — and evil. Only once before had I had sensed such blackness and evil in the mind of

22

a human. It was in the mind of the human called Jim that had killed my former master[14].

"Let's move to one side," she said, "and see if we can get a better look."

I understood the essence of her words, and we tried working our way further left and forward. As we did, I realized that she wanted to be able to see what the two men looked like from the front.

Most of the crowd had stopped flowing by this time, and had become a large number of people standing or milling around, as if waiting for something.

That made it easier for us to change position, and we had just about flanked them when one of the men strode off towards the large fire that was burning inside a circle of box-shaped rocks.

***

I was surprised to see Silver pick up a scent, or perhaps a sense, of something that concerned him. Although he had many other skills and qualities, he had been specifically trained to detect explosives. The front lawn of the Parliament Buildings seemed like an unlikely place for someone to be carrying explosives, but with so many people crowded together it wouldn't take much of an explosion to do a lot of harm, so I gave him his head and followed along, trying to look everywhere at once.

Having worked his way through the crowd and focused in on what was concerning him, he eventually came to a complete standstill and just stood there. He seemed to be staring at two men that were just ahead of us. One was quite large, with a shock of rather unruly-looking dark hair and the other quite ordinary – about medium height and medium build - in fact, the only really distinguishing feature of the second man was that he had blond hair.

I could see that the fur on the back of Silver's neck was standing up and I thought I detected a quiver in his body, so I knelt down for a closer look.

"Something wrong?" I asked, quietly. "Is it those two men?"

"Grrruph," he said, in acknowledgement, but quietly – as if not wanting to be overheard.

This was unusual. If he had smelled explosives, or even the

chemical precursors used to make explosives, he would have simply walked up to the source, sat down on his haunches, and looked up at me to signal his find. But he hadn't done any of those things.... Something else then, but what?

Then I looked into his eyes and got a sense of *darkness*, it seemed like, and *menace*, and I could feel his body shaking. I'd only seen him react like this one other time – when he'd met Jim Dumont, a hunting and fishing guide in northern Saskatchewan. I hadn't known how to interpret Silver's reaction then, but Jim had turned out to be a murderer and thief! I wasn't about to discount Silver's instincts a second time.

Silver and I moved to one side and worked our way around, trying to get a view from the front so I could see what the two men's faces looked like.

We just had a glimpse, before the larger man stepped away, strode purposefully up to the Centennial Flame and hopped up on the low stone wall that surrounded it. He had a bullhorn in his hand.

Quickly slipping my daypack off, I took out my camera and looked at it. Not much of a surveillance camera, I thought. The only camera I owned at that time was the Kodak Pocket Instamatic camera I'd purchased as a university student. Its virtues had been its low price, small size, and the fact that I could afford to buy the Ikelite underwater housing for it that allowed me to take pictures while SCUBA diving. The small, cheap lens and '110' roll film it used didn't lend themselves to high-resolution photographs, but they produced acceptable slide transparencies and 4 x 6" prints.

In this case, it did look like the kind of camera an impoverished university student might own, so I used it to take a picture of the man with the bullhorn. Then, edging closer to the Centennial Flame, as if eager to hear what the man had to say, I kept an eye on the blond-haired man, watching for a chance to see him from the front.

When there was a gap and I could see his face, I snapped as many pictures as I could while holding the camera at chest height, hoping that if spotted I would look like I was waiting for the right moment to take another picture of the speaker.

When the crowd settled, the man with the bullhorn began to speak. Between the garbled sound of his amplified voice and his tendency to swing the bullhorn back and forth, right and left, it wasn't easy to understand everything he said but I could pick out the sense of it. He was arguing for an end to seal hunting in Canada's northern and eastern coasts, and calling for people to step up and demand action from the federal government. I had seen a number of people carrying banners and signs. Now they brandished them above their heads. Some of them had graphic colour pictures of Harp Seal pups, lying dead and bleeding on the snow and ice, with words like '**Stop the Murder**,' and so on.

That helped explain the location for the crowd's gathering: right in front of the Parliament Buildings.

Watching Silver, I tried to figure out which of the two men was the focus of his attention, but I got a surprise. It was both of them. His body would stiffen, as would the fur on the back of his neck, when he looked at 'bullhorn man,' and also when he looked at 'blond-haired man.' The only difference was that he'd sometimes give a low growl when gazing at the blond-haired man.

I decided to look for a better vantage point and signalled to Silver that we should continue moving to our left. As we did so, the bullhorn man seemed to wrap-up his remarks and, with an ever-increasing note of hysteria in his voice, called for the crowd to march on and make their voices heard.

Heard by whom? I wondered.

As the crowd shifted, Silver and I went with the flow for a while. While the bullhorn man was leading the crowd out the main gate and back onto Wellington Street, the people near us seemed to know where he was heading, and we were swept past the West Block of the Parliament Buildings, and eastward towards the Chateau Laurier Hotel.

Walking down the street with the crowd we found ourselves, for a moment, at the head of the crowd. This happened because those around us had slowed down to wait for their leader, with the bullhorn, and the advance guard of banner and protest sign bearers, to catch up and take the lead.

Taking a moment to look around, it was only then that I saw the police line!

Perhaps 30 or 40 metres (30–40 yards) away, a police line stretched from just before the Chateau Laurier, to our left, all the way across Wellington Street, to the Government Conference Centre[23] on the other side. Two things immediately flashed into my mind. One was that there were some kind of high-level meetings going on between the Prime Minister and the Provincial Premiers, and their respective entourages of Cabinet Ministers and senior civil servants. The meetings were being held in the conference centre and the out-of-town politicians and civil servants were staying at the Chateau Laurier. That explained the timing and focal point of the protestors.

The second thing that imposed itself on my mind was the police line. A mixture of RCMP and Ottawa City Police officers were assembled, but this was no ordinary police line with rolls of yellow tape instructing people not to cross. This was a huge turnout. It stretched out all the way across one of Wellington Street's broadest intersections, and was at least six officers deep at any point. Furthermore, the front line of officers, facing towards the advancing protestors, were fully outfitted in riot gear.

I have to admit that my first reaction was fascination, as I assessed the deployment of the police resources to my left and then the sheer size of noisy protesters heading towards me from the right.

My fascination was heightened even further when I heard the throaty-engine sounds of a very large diesel engine approaching.

What in the world? I wondered.

The engine noise sounded louder and louder as something mechanical approached from behind the police line. Then, just as I heard the sound of the engine changing gears, I saw a long nozzle appear above the police line, which blurred for a moment as officers in the centre of the line shuffled aside to make room. Then the rest of it appeared.

They had brought in one of the huge greenish-yellow-coloured, crash-tender fire-engines from the Ottawa Airport!

Only then did it dawn on me that Silver and I were not standing in a smart place to be. The police line was clearly well staffed, well equipped, and bracing for violence. They certainly weren't going to need help from us.

Looking them over, I could see that they were prepared to elevate their response according to the "use of force" doctrine[8]. This means employing only the amount of force necessary to achieve the specific mission. When applied to riots, this would proceed as follows:

1. A show of force,

2.   The use of riot control formations to halt or drive a mob, and/or to split it into manageable groups,
3.   The use of high-pressure water to disperse the mob,
4.   The use of riot control agents, like tear gas[24], to disperse the mob,
5.   Fire by sharpshooters to render the mob's leadership ineffective, and
6.   The use of full-unit firepower when all else has failed.

The police line in front of us had implemented the first two of these, the presence of the fire truck meant they were prepared to deploy number three, and they would certainly have come prepared to advance, if necessary, to number four. Number five had been rarely used in North America, although most people still remembered the 1970 Vietnam War protests in which protesting students were either shot or bayonetted by troops.

In the demonstration I was facing, the protestors were resolutely, and noisily, advancing – being egged-on by bullhorn man and their own rising adrenaline. They were showing no signs of being intimidated by the police line, much less their obvious show of willingness to turn a high-pressure water cannon on them.

As I belatedly realized that we were going to be caught dead centre between two resolute forces, I decided that we should make our way out while we could, and certainly before the police starting firing tear gas and smoke cannisters!

Fortunately, the people near us were still waiting for the leaders to catch up, and Silver and I were able to get off of the street, back up onto the Parliament Hill Grounds, and then make our exit along the front of the East Block.

So much for our Sunday 'walk in the park.'

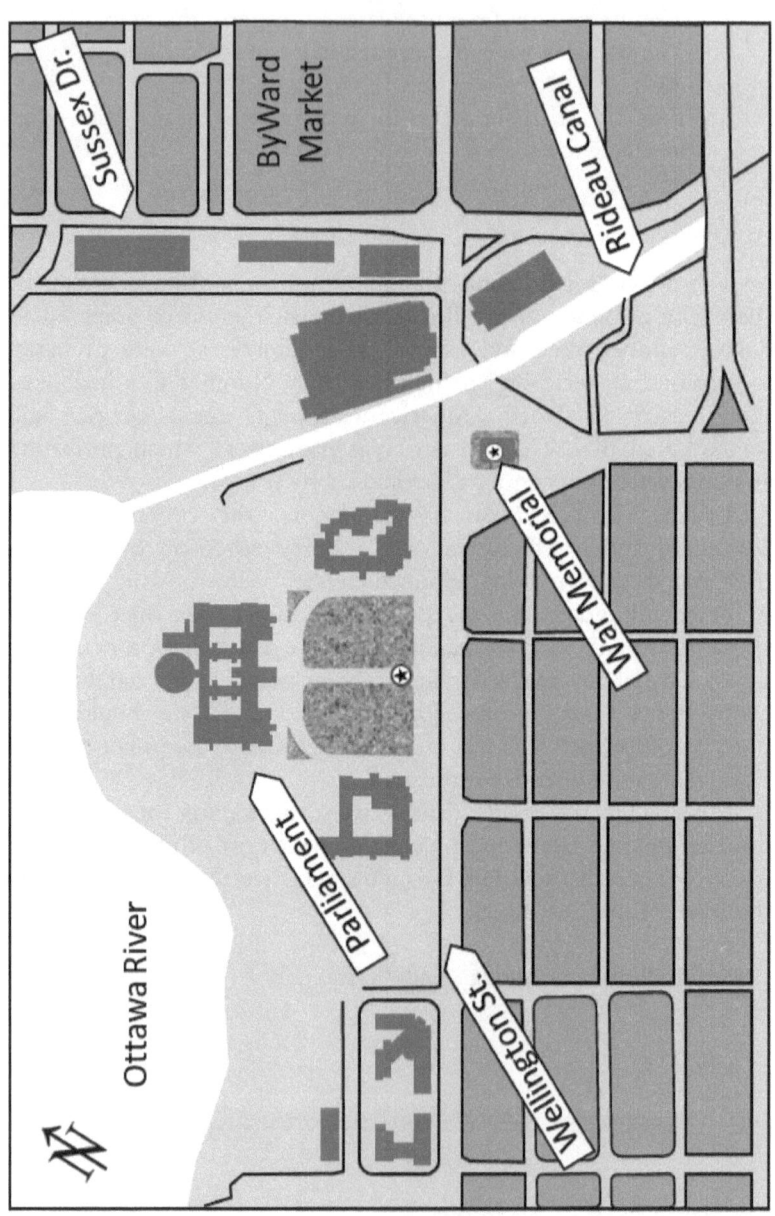

The rioter has changed from the hurler of brickbats to the thrower of dynamite bombs.

Unknown Military Author
20ᵗʰ Century

Back at work, the next morning, I related my story of finding myself between the protesters and the riot squad to my boss, Staff Sergeant Bob Simpson. He was naturally interested in our mystery person, citing concerns that violent agitators seemed to be infiltrating the seal hunt protesters who were otherwise peacefully demonstrating with occasional lapses into mild civil disobedience.

"We're not concerned with the law-abiding protesters," he said, "and any minor transgressions are for the local police to deal with, but the violent ones are a concern for two reasons: one, for the damage they can do, and two, because their actions can encourage others that might normally be peaceful and law-abiding but get caught up in the heat of the moment and follow the example set by the instigators. In the worst cases, it can lead to outright riots."

"Who are the instigators then?" I asked, "anarchists?"

"Sometimes, yes, people that want to bring down all of society's organized systems to make room for a new kind of society."

"I've always wondered what anarchists would do if they succeeded. Would they then shift to rebelling against whatever kind of new government and society came next?" I asked.

"I really don't know," said Bob, "anarchists have always struck me as short-term thinkers. I can understand their frustrations and anger, but it's *naïve* to think that you can bring a system down and not have some kind of new one grow-up in its place. Sometimes I think they're like dogs chasing cars: the chase is all well and good but what would a dog do with a car once it caught it?

"Anyway, there are several other types of violent instigators beside anarchists: foreign agents attempting to undermine our political system, for example, and *provocateurs* hired by a third party."

"Hired?"

"Sure. Remember the student protests in the United States during the Vietnam War?"

"Yes. I met a few American students in university that had fled here to avoid the draft. Some of them had been beaten by the police for simply being part of a crowd of demonstrators. Between their anger at the war and their disenchantment at being attacked by their own police, they'd come to Canada vowing never to return to the U.S."

"Well, the FBI think that some of the more violent clashes between the students and police were incited by *provocateurs* that had been hired to goad the police and national guard into retaliating with excessive force, causing the demonstrators to respond with violence - leading to injuries, property destruction, intense media coverage, and even deaths."

This was a new thought for me. "Who would do that... and why?"

"I don't know, but it wasn't just American students that were against the war. There were many others that were against it but unwilling to be seen to disagree publicly, some of them quite wealthy. The FBI think that there may have been people that felt that if the student demonstrations could be turned into violent confrontations, especially if there were injuries and deaths, then the horror of seeing government forces acting against their own citizens would lead to further demonstrations, and that eventually the general public would turn against the war, causing the government to pull its troops out of Vietnam."

That triggered memories. "Four students were killed at Kent State...."

"In 1970, yes, and nine others were shot and injured. Within a week, nearly a dozen students were bayonetted at demonstration at the University of New Mexico, and within a week of that more students were killed or injured at Jackson State University[25]."

"And you think that the more violent clashes were triggered by these *provocateurs*?

"I don't know. Neither does the FBI, they just have suspicions. Even if their general suspicions are correct, the instigators could just as easily have been foreign agents. North Vietnam, China, and the Soviet Union would all have wanted to see the American public turn against the war."

"And now you think Silver and I might have accidentally come across one of these *provocateurs* yesterday?"

"The thought crossed my mind, that's all," said Bob. "Maybe

we got a lucky break…. Let's wait and see whether any of your pictures turned out. If so, we'll have a search done and see if anything comes up. In the meantime, why don't you do some reading up on the seal hunt protests. We might want you and Silver to go sniff around a few more of their protests – but carefully."

I'd noticed that since being promoted to Corporal[26], Bob seemed to be giving me more latitude to follow my own instincts and choose, or even suggest, some of the cases that I took on. This was the latest example. It meant shouldering more responsibility, but it felt good.

After my talk with Bob, it was time to do some research, so I headed over to the library at Carleton University to see what I could dig up. After an afternoon's poring through a dozen articles and a half dozen books, I'd learned that seal hunting in the eastern Arctic region predates the arrival of Viking and European explorers, and that it originally provided food and clothing for the Inuit peoples in the far northeast. It became a source of revenue when the European Sealing Fleets arrived in the 1700s. By the 1800s, it was a major industry, particularly in Newfoundland and Labrador. Modern-era, commercial sealing began in the 1930s, when Norwegian sealers began arriving, and these were soon joined by Canadian commercial sealers. The commercial sealers were mostly after the seals' pelts, and prized among these were the pure white pelts of each season's young harp seal pups – 'whitecoats.' Although the Canadian Government began regulating the hunts in the 1950s, this did nothing to satisfy the people that wanted to see an outright ban on commercial seal hunting.

In the 1960s, came the first wave of protests sponsored by organized animal and environmental conservation groups, who also began to directly lobby politicians regarding their opposition to the seal hunts in Canada[27] (and Norway). Their major weapons in such campaigns were explicit, colour photographs and documentary films showing cute, white seal pups being clubbed to death by commercial sealers interested only in their pelts.

All of the above tended to be well covered by the media, particularly the newspapers and television. It was television, in fact, that led to the first wave of public reaction. In 1964, the CBC French network aired a documentary film that contained particularly graphic scenes of violence against the seals, including one that showed a seal being skinned alive[28]. Although the hunter concerned latter admitted to being paid to stage the scene precisely to create a horrifying image, the documentary was very effective at stimulating public outrage.

I also found some magazine and newspaper articles about the protest movements themselves. Not long after the CBC documentary film was aired, the International Alliance for Animal Protection[29] (IAAP) was founded, based in Fredericton, NB. Although generally opposed to the killing or inhumane treatment of any animals, limited resources forced them to focus on only a few specific initiatives at any one time. Of these, the annual seal hunts quickly became a priority for action. Most of the initial activities involved advertising to raise public awareness and lobbying of governments and industries, all using the opportunities presented by the graphic photographs and films which could so easily be shown as direct evidence on placards and mailers, and in newspapers and television.

In particular, IAAP focused on large-vessel sealing operations. The efforts of IAAP, and similar organizations had an impact. By the mid-1970s, the Canadian government had brought in new regulations, including setting quotas, licensing of sealers and their vessels, and prohibiting the skinning of live seals. The organizations, and a significant fraction of the international public, weren't satisfied, however, with the extent of the regulations and the perceived lack of enforcement of them. These concerns were only compounded when a government appointed Committee on Seals and Sealing called for a phase-out of the Canadian and Norwegian seal hunts by 1974[30], but their recommendation was ignored.

Meanwhile, the proliferation of colour television in households across the country provided an ideal medium to show graphic, heart-rending pictures and movie clips of the bloody seal hunts to a broad audience. This fueled increased public interest and outrage with another wave of protests surging in the mid-1970s. The protests themselves were boosted by the participation of movie stars. In March 1977, activists had been able to fly-in French actress Brigitte Bardot, and the cover of the next edition of *Paris Match* featured a picture of her hugging a whitecoat seal pup[31]. This helped the controversy spread to Europe.

When I next met with Bob to discuss what I'd learned, we

talked about the police-related aspects of the protests.

"The organized protests, for the most part, have been conducted legally as legitimate expressions of public opinion," he explained. "In these cases, the only matters of concern to us are the minority of protesters that step 'over the line' into illegal activities… and it's not just the protesters," he pointed out. "We've had cases of counter-protesters that just as angrily condemn the protesters and sometimes they cross the line too."

Counter-protesters, in the case of sealing, were usually made up of the sealers themselves, plus members of their families and/or residents of communities that were dependent on the seal hunt. There were already instances in which some of these had taken violent exception to what they viewed as the protesters threatening their livelihoods.

"That raises another concern," continued Bob, "which is that if violence breaks out on both sides. Things could escalate into a riot.

"The real concerns for us, though, are the activist protesters who, as the name implies, are not content with public awareness and diplomacy, and who turn to more direct ways to accomplish the changes they want. Although some of these people confine themselves to perfectly legal means, such as protest marches, we've seen others purposely tread 'across the line' into barricades and even physical disruption of the seal hunts. We suspect that even the larger organizations, like the IAAP, are becoming dissatisfied with what they perceive to be an almost complete lack of progress with government, and may be considering ways to impede the sealing operations directly."

"Aren't they doing that already?" I asked. "I thought I read somewhere that one of these groups recently took a ship right onto the ice pack and had a bunch of protesters rush out onto the ice a spray the seal pups with coloured dye, hoping to save them by making their pelts useless for making clothing."

"Yes, but we're worried that they might get impatient enough to create even more media attention by hiring professional agitators to incite and inflame things."

"Ah hah. Like our mystery man from the Parliament Hill protest march."

"Exactly."

I'd read a bit about this too. Generally unknown to the media or the public at large, there had been disturbing indications of the involvement of professional agitators in some mass demonstrations of the 1960s and 1970s.

"What kind of people are these professional agitators?" I asked.

"Mercenaries. Usually, they are ex-military or ex-police that have been dishonourably discharged or otherwise weeded out, but who have found that their lack of ethics combined with their military or police training are in demand. They bring with them the tools of professional anarchy: fighting tactics, weapons, and explosives."

I must have made a face, as I was thinking about Bob's words, because he next spoke a bit more sharply.

"Don't underestimate these people Alex. They lack integrity, and maybe even humanity, but they are generally well trained, experienced, and motivated. Within the context of what they're hired to do, some of them are quite intelligent and even professional. Others are deranged but very cunning.... Some of them are killers."

"Riiiiight," I said. *Nasty*, I thought.

I had an unsettling feeling that the mystery man Silver and I had encountered might be one of these professional agitators. Now, I would have to try digging deeper...

***

The next development was with the pictures I'd taken (no pun intended). As predicted, the 4 x 6" prints from my small camera were anything but high-resolution. Nevertheless, one shot of bullhorn man was very clear and several of the head-and-shoulders shots of the blond-haired man were very good.

It wasn't long before Bob, had news about them.

"The man with the bullhorn has been identified as the President, and one of the founders, of the International Alliance for Animal Protection and he lives in Fredericton, where the IAAP has their main office. His name is Arne Kristiansen. He's well known in the animal rights movements internationally, and pops up in the news media now and again. IAAP is a legitimate not-for-profit organization, and as far as we know both IAAP and Kristiansen have been law abiding and not a police concern. It was the IAAP that organized the demonstration you two walked into."

"How about the blond-haired man?"

"Your other man is a bit of a mystery. We tried running his photo through CPIC[32] but no match came up...." Bob gave his Cheshire Cat smile.

"And?" I prompted. I could tell there was more coming.

"Well, as you know, CPIC is linked to the U.S. National Crime Information Center."

"Right, NCIC."

"Mm hmm. Do you remember Deputy Director Jonathan Wheeler, of the FBI?"

"Sure, I met him after the Aleutian Islands incident[20] and then again after Soviet satellite incident[18]."

"Right. Well the U.S. system passed a null response back to CPIC, but I received a phone call from Jon Wheeler the next day. Turns out our query did match one of their records, but the record is classified Top Secret. Even though we didn't get a useful response from the computer system, the fact that there was a query and a match raised a flag that was sent to the FBI."

"Wow. OK, so he's known to the Americans but they're protecting his identity because of some kind of security concern. Did he tell you what it is?"

"Nope. He wanted to know why we were interested, and when I explained he said they were very interested but he wouldn't tell me why. Not even over a STEW phone[33]."

"Has that ever happened before?"

"Not to my knowledge. If you've stumbled onto something so hot that they won't even trust a secure telephone, then they're seriously worried about something."

"So that's it then – we've hit a brick wall?"

"Oh no, not at all. Jon wouldn't talk about it over the phone, but he's sending Vivian up to meet with you. They'd like to hear your story firsthand, and in return she'll brief you on what they know and why they're interested." His Cheshire smile returned. "I don't think they're protecting him at all.... I think they're trying to find him."

***

A few days later, Special Agent Vivian Rule flew in on a commercial flight. Silver and I went to meet her at the Ottawa airport. I was in uniform, as Silver and I had just been outside the city helping with a search for a lost child (fortunately, it turned out to be a false alarm).

"Where are you staying?" I asked, while we waited for her luggage to be delivered to the carousel.

"Some hotel downtown," she replied, "I'll have to look up the reservation."

"Why not cancel it and come stay with Silver and me? It will be more comfortable and easier for us to talk. I'd like to hear all about what you've been up to lately."

"Thank you, yes, that sounds great," she replied, "I'd like to hear how things are coming along with you too, and how you got the corporal's stripes I see on your sleeve."

Vivian is about my age, and was one of the first two women to become Special Agents in the FBI. She's brunette, fairly tall, slender, and has wonderful, large brown eyes. We'd found, on previous assignments, that we worked well together, and we'd become friends as well.

Settled in at my place, we only chatted about things like what each of us had been doing outside of work in the month – *had it only been a month?* - since we'd worked together in the Northwest Territories[18], above the Arctic Circle. Vivian had just come back from an exciting vacation in Europe, and wanted to know how things had been going with my boyfriend Don, who was in military intelligence and a colleague of ours.

After dinner, we sat out on my back porch watching one of Ottawa's classic evening thunderstorms roll across the sky. The cracks of lightning followed by rolls of thunder provided a perfect backdrop for Vivian's story.

"We've been watching a pattern lately that has emerged from quite a few of the big demonstrations in our larger cities," she began.

"You mean like the anti-war protests?"

"Yes those, but also demonstrations for women's rights, human rights generally, and even animal rights – like anti-whaling for example. Activist demonstrations are becoming normal now, which is fine as far as free speech and all that. The local police have to deal with crowd control and the rowdy fringe elements - and we sometimes get called in to investigate hate crimes – but something new has emerged.

"Tensions can run high, of course, with demonstrators

throwing bricks and bottles and such at the police, and the police hurling tear gas at the protestors. The strange thing is that at some demonstrations, just when the tensions on both sides are right at the tipping point – where one small thing could tip the balance between calming the crowd or a full-fledged riot, there's a gunshot that causes an immediate reaction from the police and surge of rioting from the demonstrators."

"You mean like when an officer gets carried away and fires into the crowd?"

"That has certainly happened before, and more than once, but I'm talking about cases where the shot came from the demonstrators' side. The first couple of times it happened, we thought they were just random incidences of armed hotheads getting carried away, but we have a forensic psychologist on staff that specializes in crowd psychology and riots. She's been looking at the demonstrations that weren't exactly peaceful, but weren't expected to turn into riots. Her goal is to come up with ways to de-escalate crowd violence before the police have to resort to water cannons, tear gas, and rubber bullets. She's the one that found this pattern, and she thinks that there's someone out there doing the exact opposite."

"You mean watching a crowd, judging the critical moment, and doing something to escalate the violence?"

"Exactly. I can see from your expression that you find it hard to believe."

"Well, it seems like a stretch. How sure are you that it's not just a series of coincidences?"

"We aren't sure, but let me lay out a few things. The demonstrations that unexpectedly turned into riots seem to have begun with the anti-war demonstrations at Kent State University in May 1970."

"That's the one where four students were killed."

"Right, and it led to violent clashes at other universities in the following weeks[25]. That was eight years ago. Since the war ended, we've had six other demonstrations, for other causes, but that seem to fit the same pattern."

"OK," I said, thinking about it, "and you and your psychologist think that some person or some organization is inciting the shifts to violence.... It still sounds a bit crazy to me. If these demonstrations have been for different causes then what's the common factor? You think it's anarchists?"

"Not exactly. There's a second part of the pattern, and this takes us to the really secret part of my story."

"Ah hah, let me refill your wine glass," I said, topping up our glasses.

Suitably restored with a sip of wine, Vivian continued. "After each of the seven demonstrations we've identified in the U.S. that fit the pattern, the police or security people have found a particular kind of gun left at the scene. In each case the gun was found lying close to what would have been the front line of the crowd of demonstrators."

"What kind of gun?"

"It's called a Deer Gun. Here, I'll show you." Getting up, Vivian went into the house to get her briefcase. Bringing it outside, she opened it and withdrew a glossy black and white photograph of a rather ugly looking little pistol.

"Home-made?" I asked.

"Not home-made. Cheaply made. It's a single-shot pistol, although it's made to carry extra rounds in the grip, and they're designed to be used once then thrown away."

"A disposable pistol. OK, why?"

Vivian sighed. "They were made for the CIA in the 1960s. I gather the idea was to provide them to guerrilla or revolutionary forces that the U.S. might be supporting in overseas countries. The soldiers there would use them to kill enemy troops and then arm themselves with the enemy's weapons. The CIA codenamed them Deer Guns, and they were cheap to make – mostly aluminum and plastic, and costing about $4 each!"

"Are they easy to get? I mean like on the black market or whatever."

"Actually no, they aren't. That's another strange thing. There were only a thousand of them ever made. 150 of them were sent to South Vietnam during the war and then the program was abruptly halted and all of them were ordered destroyed. The CIA says they are confident that the 850 that were never deployed were properly destroyed, but it's a little less certain that all of the 150 in Vietnam were destroyed."

"Why's that?"

"They had been sent to the army's Special Forces. We were able to check the army's disposal records, which contain a receipt showing that all 150 of them were sent for destruction. The signature on the receipt shows that the guns were received by a Major Davy Jones...." She paused for effect.

"*CRACK!*" There was a loud crack of lightning, almost immediately followed by a roar of thunder and it started to rain. There was a roof over my deck, so we didn't have to move but it certainly happened at the right time to add some drama to Vivian's story.

"Major David Jones, U.S. Special Forces was the cover name for a CIA officer operating in South Vietnam, but he had been listed as MIA[34] after a battle with the North Vietnamese several months earlier. It was thought that he died in a helicopter crash, although no body was ever found. Neither was the helicopter."

"Who was it then? No, let me guess. Major Jones was still alive and it was the CIA that quietly took them back."

"Maybe. The CIA aren't prone to giving up their secrets, even to the FBI, so it's difficult to be sure about anything. But in this case, we suspect that the man known as Major Jones caused his own disappearance and struck out on his own as a mercenary, taking the guns with him and probably the helicopter too."

"And you think he was hired as a professional agitator for the demonstrations you listed, and that each time he used one of these Deer Guns and then left it behind as a kind of calling card."

"That's exactly what we think. The guns are untraceable, and our forensic psychologist thinks it's some kind of ego thing for him to leave them behind. Taunting us, if you like. Challenging us to find and catch him, even."

"OK then, don't take this the wrong way, but why haven't you caught him then? I assume he must have been seen at some of the demonstrations?"

"First of all, if you piece together all the eyewitness accounts you might conclude that it was a different person each time. Different heights, different builds, different clothes. But it could have been the same person in each case, wearing disguises. He wouldn't be able to artificially lower his height, but he could easily raise it. The rest could be done with wigs, makeup, and different clothes and accessories."

"So, he's good with disguises."

"Better than good. Did you happen to read about the women's

rights demonstration in downtown Toronto back in March of this year?"

"The one where the police fired on the crowd and were hammered in the press for shooting at unarmed mothers and grandmothers?"

"That's the one. Apparently, things only got out of hand when someone threw two Molotov Cocktails into the police ranks. Except they weren't your everyday, spur of the moment Molotovs. According to the forensic report, they were a pretty fancy self-igniting kind – no need to do anything obvious like light the wicks, and they had been disguised as ordinary beer bottles. Several of the demonstrators told the police that they had seen a grey-haired woman take a beer bottle out of a large purse or shoulder bag and throw it over the police line. Part of the reason it stuck in their memories was that the woman had such a strong throwing arm!"

"And was there a shot from the crowd?"

"There was. A single shot was heard by the same people that remembered the grey-haired woman, and a police officer was struck in the leg by a slug from a 9 mm gun."

"I suppose the Deer Guns fired 9 mm rounds?"

"Right again, and a Deer Gun was found lying on the ground less than ten feet from the front of the police line in Toronto."

"You obviously suspect your Major Jones."

"Yes. Same MO[35], same results, same kind of gun. The only new twist was the Molotovs, but even those were the work of someone with specialized knowledge. From the witness reports, our mystery person was tall enough and stocky enough. Add the wig and glasses, put on a full-length dress - you know, she even wore a shawl! - and there you have our man in disguise rather than someone's grandmother."

"So, the Toronto demonstration gives you eight that fit your pattern?"

"That we know of. He's a killer, Alex. A couple of Deer Guns have also been found near the scene of assassinations in third-world countries. It's possible that they're not connected, but we think it's the same person and that he's sometimes hired himself out as a paid assassin." She sighed, and then changed the subject. "How about telling me about your Ottawa demonstration?"

I told Vivian about Silver's and my experience at the Ottawa demonstration, and the photos I'd taken.

"Can I see the photos?" she asked.

"Sure, I have copies for you," and I went to get them for her.

When I returned, I explained that the one I thought of as bullhorn man had been identified, but it was the other one that had her full attention.

"I think he's finally made a mistake," she said thoughtfully.

Going back to her briefcase, she withdrew a different file folder and opened it. Taped onto the inside cover of the folder was an old, faded colour-photograph of a man wearing jungle camouflage and holding an automatic rifle. Attached to his backpack shoulder straps, where they came over his shoulders and upper chest, were a large sheath knife (mounted upside down) and a grenade. In the background was jungle. "This is him, taken in Vietnam in 1963."

"It's not very clear," I said, doubtfully, as I looked at it.

"No, but look at the hair."

The man in the picture had his hair cut short, but it was blond.

"Could be a coincidence?" I suggested.

"Sure, but maybe not. His size and age seem about right too. A young Major could have been 32 in 1963, which would make him about 47 now. Maybe he was at your demonstration to meet your bullhorn man and talk about a future job. They may have thought that meeting in the middle of a large crowd would be enough to avoid attention. If it's our elusive Major Jones then I'm sure he's travelling under a false name and passport, and probably feels quite safe and anonymous. Like 'hiding in plain sight.' That could explain why he wasn't in disguise."

"So, what's next?"

"Feel like going undercover again?"

"Maybe. What do you have in mind?"

"Well, up until now, we've only learned things about him after he's long gone. Maybe we can get ahead of him with this IAAP organization."

"You mean get inside and wait for a big demonstration that might turn violent, then try to spot him?"

"Basically. Yes."

"I don't know, Vivian. The next sealing season isn't until next March or April. I'll have to talk to Bob about it. Can I tell him what you've told me?"

"Bob yes, but no one else – and nothing in writing. OK?"

4 THE ACTRESS

July 21, 1978
Gibsons, British Columbia

Having wrapped up an unrelated case in Vancouver, Silver and I had boarded a B.C. Ferry at Horseshoe Bay, in West Vancouver, and made a very enjoyable 40-minute crossing of the Strait of Georgia. Since he is a police dog, the ship's crew allowed him to stay with me, rather than remain cooped up in the truck on the vehicle deck, so he was able to enjoy the crossing as well. It never ceases to amaze me how Silver can hate the water so much and yet enjoying boating so much – even in rough water – but he does.

Once across the strait, we drove off the ferry and into the small village of Langdale. A quick left turn took us a short distance along Marine Drive to Gibsons, a small town of a few thousand people whose current claim to fame was that it was the home setting for the popular CBC-television series *The Beachcombers*[36].

The series focused on the lives and adventures of several characters that made their living boating up and down the British Columbia coastline salvaging logs that had slipped away from logging-industry barges and booms. The hometown of the central characters in the series was this same town of Gibsons, although several of the series' buildings were studio sets, not real buildings.

The network was in the process of filming new segments, and Silver and I were there to meet one of the show's stars, a drop-dead-gorgeous blond actress and sex-symbol named Ginger

Brandt. I'd never met a movie star before and was looking forward to it.

The trailers for the actors and staff were set up in a compound on the edge of town, right near the edge of the water. This put them within easy walking distance of the town and gave them a fantastic view of the sheltered waters of the Strait of Georgia. Not wanting to disclose my occupation to these people, I only identified myself by showing my driver's licence to the guard at the security gate. Having consulted a list to verify that I was expected, the guard showed me where to park and waved in the general direction I should walk.

"Trailer number five," he said, "ask anyone if you get lost."

Each trailer had a large number taped conspicuously to its front, and they were actually arranged more or less in numerical order, so we had no trouble finding number five. It had a doorbell, and was quite promptly opened by a blond, blue-eyed woman of about my own age. It was Ginger Brandt all right.

"Yes?" she said, looking a bit stern and aloof.

"My name is Alex Houston. I have an appointment to see you."

"You're Alex Houston?" she asked. "And you're a Mountie?"

"That's right, Corporal Alexandra Houston, and this is my partner Silver."

"Really? He's a Mountie too?"

"Well, he's an RCMP police service dog, so yes, I guess he is. I never quite thought of it quite that way."

"I love animals. Can I say hi to him?"

"Sure."

Bending down on one knee, she very formally said "Hello Silver, my name's Ginger," and stretched her hand out for him to sniff.

"See how he looks into my eyes," she said, without taking her gaze away. "It's like he can see right inside my head."

"You'll think I'm crazy, but that's not far off. He's unusually perceptive, and picks up more of human conversations than any animal I've ever heard of."

"Nothing is crazier than the movie business. Well, Silver if you look deep inside, you'll see what I'm really like."

After a long look, Silver broke his gaze, took a step forward and gave her a lick on the chin.

"That's a high compliment coming from him," I said.

Ginger's demeanor had changed radically during our introductions, and now she started laughing. "Come in. Come in, and let me explain why I was a bit surprised by your appearance."

As she stepped back to wave us in, we entered a beautifully laid-out room that was a combination living room, kitchen and dining room. It was also very bright and cheerful with almost the entire ceiling having been taken over by large skylights which nourished an amazing assortment of plants.

"Like it?" she said, observing my reactions.

"I love it," I said. "It's beautiful. Like being in a conservatory."

"It's two trailers put together, actually. The second half has a bedroom, *en suite*, and an office. Behind that is a deck. Let me get you something to drink and I'll show you. What would you like?"

"Anything cold would be great. Water's fine."

"How about a Perrier for you and plain water for Silver? I'll join you."

Going to the kitchen, she extracted two large glasses and two bottles of Perrier, which she handed to me. Then, she filled a bowl with water, motioned with a nod of her head and led me out to her back deck.

The deck was quite private, having solid walls on each side and a translucent roof. The view was fantastic. We were just high enough to have an unobstructed view of the ocean and, across the straight to the eastern coast of Vancouver Island.

"Pretty great view, huh?" she said, watching me closely.

"It's amazing. I love being on the coast. Either coast."

As we settled into comfortable deck loungers, she brought the conversation back to business.

"Bob didn't tell me he was sending a woman to see me, he just said it would be one of his people, name of Alex Houston...."

"Yes, my formal name is Alexandra but everyone calls me Alex. I hope you will too."

"And you really work for Bob Simpson?"

I nodded. "You know what he does for a living, right?"

"Yes, but I didn't know the RCMP was letting women in."

"There aren't many of us yet. They started with me as a single-woman pilot project in 1974, then an entire troop of women in 1975, and now there are more and more each year."

"So you were the first! That must have been hard."

"There have been a few rough spots, but not as many as you

might think. Not for me anyway. Between my undercover work and being a dog handler, I get a lot of independence, which I love, and I think that by not being in any of the larger detachments or sub-divisions I haven't really been seen as a challenge to anyone."

"Well good for you. I like to see women get ahead and not just because of their looks." She looked at me knowingly. "I imagine you're wondering how I know Bob."

"You know, I was actually wondering how it is that Bob knows a movie star."

"Well, that part's easy. He's my uncle – on my mother's side. He called and said he needed my help and it would be for a cause I believe in. He said he'd be sending two of his best officers, and that they would explain...." Then, she laughed. "Call me out of touch, but I expected to see two men, not a woman and a dog."

"Yes, that sounds like Bob's sense of humour. Here's the thing, we're after a killer that hires himself out as a professional agitator. He'll slip into a group of angry demonstrators, wait until tensions between them and the police are near the boiling point and then initiate the first moves of real violence."

"Initiate how?"

"In many cases, he uses disposable guns to shoot someone like a police officer. Sometime he uses explosives. Then when things on both sides tip out of control he slips away, leaving behind one of his disposable guns as a kind of calling card."

"You said 'he.' Do you know who he is?"

"Not for sure, and it could be a woman, but the methods this person uses match those of an ex-CIA officer gone rogue that the FBI have been after for years now. One of the trademark guns was found after a women's-rights demonstration in Toronto that turned violent. Whomever it is, they seem to be a master of disguise. Silver and I got involved in this because we were bystanders at a 'save the seals' demonstration in Ottawa earlier in the month. Silver reacted so strongly to the presence of two men that we followed them for a few minutes and I was able to unobtrusively take their pictures. One of them turned out to look like the man that the FBI thinks is the one they're after."

"What do you mean Silver reacted?"

"Ah. That's hard to explain. I mentioned that he's unusually perceptive. Well, several times now he's reacted strongly to people that later turned out to be evil, killers even. I didn't understand it, or even believe it, at first but it's happened too many times for me to ignore. When he reacted to the two men we saw in Ottawa, I followed his lead. One man is the one we were talking about. The other is the head of an organization called IAAP. That stands for International…"

"Alliance for Animal Protection, I know. You're talking about Arne Kristiansen."

"That's right. Do you know him?"

"No, but I know of him. It's becoming common for movie stars to support 'causes' and I'm no exception. In my case, the causes are animal rights: everything from prevention of cruelty to animals in general, to saving the whales, to saving the seals. I've been a supporter of IAAP for quite a while now…. I think I'm starting to see what Bob has come up with in that devious little mind of his. You want me to get attached to one of these animal rights demonstrations and help you find this bad guy, right?"

I must have looked as nonplussed as I felt, because she continued right on.

"You're surprised to find out that I have a brain, aren't you? No, don't bother to deny it. It's a very natural reaction. I know how people look at me: 'All boobs and no brains,' they think. If I do a great job of acting, hardly anyone notices, and if I do a lousy job no one cares all that much as long as I look good. It's my own fault for building a career playing roles that call for an empty-headed piece of sexy eye-candy."

I couldn't help but ask "Why do it then?"

"Well, money at first. When I started modelling it was just a job. I didn't like it though, so when I got a chance to try acting in a TV series, I jumped at it. The TV series led to movies, which are all right, but acting in a TV series turned out to be something I really love doing. In *The Beachcombers*, the director is fantastic, the cast and crew are great, and because we work together so much, we've become kind of a second family. Have you ever watched it?"

"Sure."

"OK, then you know that the character I play is 'thick as a post,' as the saying goes. That's OK, because I love the work, and it's starting to bring me opportunities to play better roles, and I'm hoping to branch out a bit. My agent is negotiating a guest appearance on *Charlie's Angels*[37] that would cast me playing a private detective that looks like a 'dumb blonde' but isn't."

"Sounds great. I hope you get it."

"Thanks, but we seem to have wandered from the point of your visit. Why don't we have lunch, and then you can tell me what it is that you and Bob want me to do?"

"Sounds great to me." I agreed.

"OK then, I'll ask my assistant to get us something. The Crafty Table makes food and snacks available for the cast and crew all day." Reaching for an extension phone that was on a nearby table she called her assistant. "Brittany, would you be a dear and pick up some lunch from the Crafty for my guests and I? I'll have my usual salad," she placed her hand over the mouthpiece and turned to me. "What would you like? They'll have salads, sandwiches, hot dogs, chips, …"

"A sandwich and some kind of diet pop would be great for me."

"How about for Silver?"

"He used to be a sled dog, so he can eat almost anything, but he loves hot dogs."

"OK. Brittany? My guest would like a sandwich and diet pop. Would you pick out a couple of kinds of each for her? And she has a dog. He'd like a couple of hot dogs, OK? We'll have them out on the deck. Thanks!"

"There you go, Brittany will bring it all over for us." Then she looked at me expectantly.

"We think that the IAAP is likely to be planning a major demonstration against the seal hunt," I began. "We know that they haven't been as successful as they'd hoped at stopping the hunting of baby harp seals. They've tried going out and dying the fur of the seal pups to destroy its commercial value, but that's been mostly a symbolic gesture as they can't dye all of the pups before being stopped by the hunters or the police. Similarly, the demonstration that Silver and I accidentally encountered in Ottawa recently got them some publicity but no real action from the federal government."

"What do you think they're going to try next then?"

"Something more dramatic. Maybe even something drastic. If we're right that this ex-CIA mercenary was meeting with the head of the IAAP in Ottawa, then it was probably about hiring him to catalyze violence."

"Where do I come in?"

"Well, I'd like to try joining the IAAP under cover and going out with them on the next protest demonstration, which we think will be in the spring during the main seal hunting season. The IAAP seem to have formed some kind of alliance with the Ocean Saviour Society, so they can use their ship – the *MV Ocean Saviour* – to get out to the ice pack off the Labrador coast."

"Ah ha! You want me to volunteer to join the protest. They'll want me to come along as a publicity stunt, and you would be able to come along as my assistant – right?"

"That's our idea exactly. What do you think?"

"I like it. I'm always looking for new things to do to contribute to the animal rights movements and this one sounds like fun. It's a natural extension of things I've done before, so it won't look suspicious. I'll get my agent to contact them about it, and if they press him, he can tell them that it will be as much a publicity stunt for me as it will for them."

"Will you be able to bring me along as your assistant?"

"Of course. We stars are so spoiled and helpless that we can't be expected to function without our personal assistants." She flashed a brilliant smile. "And naturally we'll make them pay all of our expenses. It's the least they can do."

"Ah, there is one more thing...."

"You want to bring Silver along, don't you?"

"I do. Besides being my partner, it was he that identified this dangerous fellow in the first place, and even a master of disguises won't be able to fool Silver."

At this point, she surprised me by turning to face Silver. "What about you Silver. Do you want to come with us to help save the baby seals?"

"Grrruph!" he said, looking directly into her eyes.

"How much of this does he understand?" she asked in amazement.

"I really don't know, but he knows some of the words and he has the most amazing ability to sense the essence of what people are thinking, especially when you can make direct eye contact."

"Right then, Silver comes too."

"Just like that?" I asked, somewhat unbelievingly.

"If you want to be a star, you have to act like a star," she said, pontifically. "People expect stars to be eccentric. You wouldn't believe some of the things that actors get written into their contracts." She flashed her brilliant smile again. "My contracts, for example, specify that the producers have to keep my trailer supplied with Canadian snacks, like Smarties™ and Cheezies™. That's easy here in Canada, but you wouldn't believe how hard they are to get in the U.S. Anyway, what we'll do is have my agent say that I'm willing to join their spring crusade to Labrador, that I'll be bringing my personal assistant and her dog, and that we'll each need our own accommodations. If they put up a fuss, I'll throw a movie-star-quality tantrum and refuse to go, but they won't put up a fuss – you'll see."

"This is very good of you Ginger.... I have to tell you though, that there could be some danger. This fellow we're after is dangerous, and if violence breaks out between the protesters and the sealers, people can get hurt – even innocent by-standers."

"Thanks for the warning, but I grew up as quite the tomboy, and I'm not as helpless as I look. Besides, you and Silver will look out for me, right?"

"We'll do our best."

We were interrupted then, by Ginger's assistant Brittany who arrived with a large box from which lunch was dispensed.

As we ate, I commented on the gorgeous view.

"Yes, it's beautiful here. That's another attraction of working on this show. When we're shooting on location, I get to wake up to this view every morning. I like to sit here with my coffee at first light and watch the boats. Gibson's is the gateway to the Sunshine Coast, so there's always a stream of boats travelling up and down the Inside Passage."

"The food's great here too. How do you manage to stay so slender?"

"Salads!" she sighed. "I get as much exercise as I can fit in, but that's not much so my only other option is to watch the calories. That means lots of salads for me, and just the occasional treat of Smarties or Cheezies."

Silver's hot dogs, of course, disappeared in an instant and it didn't take long for us to eat our light lunch. It was Ginger that brought the conversation back to work.

"Bringing Silver along won't be a problem. Can I tell Brittany about you? She's going to have a lot of questions if I suddenly hire a new assistant without consulting her."

"Yes, I think you'll have to but please just say that it's a favour for your uncle, and please don't tell her until just before you leave for the East Coast. Will she be OK with being left behind for this trip?"

"Oh yes. She gets seasick, even on the car ferry! So, she'll be relieved not to have to go out on a real ship in the open ocean."

"And what, by the way, does an actor's personal assistant do exactly?"

She laughed. "That's easy. Anything the actor wants of course! But don't worry. It's menial work but it's easy work. Besides, I can take care of myself if I have to. We'll just have me send you off on some trivial errands from time to time for appearances sake."

We only had a few more minutes for small talk, before Brittany called to remind Ginger that she was due for makeup shortly. As we took our leave, I thanked her for everything: her hospitality, and her willingness to go along with our plan. "Especially since it might come to nothing. Our mystery person might not show up!"

"That's OK, it will be fun," she insisted. "A chance to do some good, a trip to Labrador, a hint of danger, and my agent's going to love the publicity angle! When he gets a response from the IAAP, I'll let you know."

As Silver and I drove back to the ferry terminal, I reflected on our meeting. Not only was it successful, I'd found Ginger to be intelligent and surprisingly nice and down-to-earth. I really liked her.

Now we just had to wait.

***

July 29, 1978
Darlington Nuclear Generating Station, Ontario

Silver and I did try attending a couple more demonstrations in hopes of spotting our quarry, but without success. Near the end of the month, for example, an anti-nuclear demonstration had been advertised for the construction site of the future Darlington Nuclear Generating Station.

The Darlington site is on the north shore of Lake Ontario, about 70 km northeast of Toronto. Although the site had been cleared and fenced, construction of the four CANDU nuclear reactors themselves hadn't even begun yet (and wouldn't officially begin until 1981). Nevertheless, Greenpeace had organized the demonstration to call for a halt to the construction on the logical assumption that there would be a better chance of stopping a nuclear power plant before construction had begun in earnest than it would when the facility was half built, let alone completed and up and running.

They chose a Saturday, and were rewarded with a clear, sunny day as over a thousand demonstrators marched on the site[38]. Silver and I simply joined the throng and let it carry us along.

There was quite a mix of people – lots of students of course, but also young families, some middle-aged people, and lots of seniors. They were quite energized, with many carrying signs and banners with slogans like **"Save our Environment," "Support Project No Nuc,"** and **"Stop Darlington."** Some of the slogans were quite creative too. My favourite one read: **"Better Active Today than Radioactive Tomorrow."** I was also struck by the mood: this wasn't an angry crowd - not yet, anyway – it was more like a bunch of people heading off to a Sunday picnic in a park. Some people were honking horns, others chanting and clapping their hands, and one person was even playing bagpipes.

In another tactic I'd never seen at a protest demonstration before, a number of the organizers – identified by conspicuous green 'Greenpeace' armbands – mingled through the crowd, effectively policing their own protesters to keep things orderly and peaceful. It worked too. There was no violence, no angry confrontations with police or security people, and only a couple of pre-planned acts of civil disobedience.

The disobedience, for the most part, was limited to trespassing on the nuclear station's construction site. In the first of these, three demonstrators staged an aerial sit-in by climbing halfway up a 56 m (185 ft) electrical transmission tower at the site, and then hung large signs and banners from their perch bearing slogans like "No Nukes," and "Stop Darlington." Although they initially vowed that they wouldn't leave until the provincial government agreed to conduct a full environmental assessment on nuclear energy and a moratorium on construction at Darlington, after a 36-hour vigil they did climb down, leaving their signs and banners on display. The three were charged with trespassing and released with a summons to appear in a local court at a later date, and seemed well content with their bargain.

In another eye-catching stunt, five demonstrators parachuted onto the site, more or less, with one parachutist getting temporarily caught-up on one of the unfinished transmission towers. Here again, the demonstrators were charged with trespassing, released with court summons, and were able to walk away with only minor injuries.

Finally, at about the same time as the parachuting a sub-group of about 60 scaled the fence and held a sit-down protest. After giving them some time to make their point and ensure that the TV crews got some good news footage of them, the police calmly moved in, arrested them, and later charged them with trespassing too.

All in all, the demonstrators, security personnel, and police officers were the most peaceful and professional that I have ever seen at a protest demonstration. Although Silver and I did our best to mingle through the whole crowd, it wasn't practical for us to get close to everyone there and neither I spotted, nor Silver smelled or sensed our quarry. Either he wasn't there, or the two sides were too calm and well-behaved for him to incite or catalyze anything violent.

At the end of the afternoon, with the vast majority of the demonstrators leaving, I decided we'd done what we could and Silver and I left as well.

That's one of the things about what people call 'good old-fashioned police work,' a lot of one's time is spent being methodical and checking for evidence, clues, and even just insights. The exciting parts, when they come, tend to be intense, sometimes even spectacular, but relatively brief.

It was quite some time before our next opportunity arose.

Laurie Schramm

5 THE ACTIVISTS CONTINUE

August 27, 1978
Sydney, Australia

A crowd had gathered for the latest protest against police intervention and actions at a Mardi Gras Parade that had been organized by Sydney's GLBTQ[39] communities as part of worldwide International Gay Solidarity Day, June 24, 1978. Although the authorities had given prior approval for the event, which included a march followed by speeches, the state police had intervened to stop the parade, confiscated the public address system, and ordered the protesters to disperse. None of these actions being well received, the protesters kept on parading and the police called in reinforcements. Eventually tensions erupted, leading to bad behaviour on both sides. Some of the 1,000 protesters shifted from singing and dancing to throwing bottles, cans, and other debris at the police. Some of the police took off their identification numbers and waded into the crowd swinging their batons at everyone they could reach. The ensuing riot lasted two hours and culminated in over fifty arrests.

Over the next two months, a series of demonstrations were held around Australia not just to appeal for sexual equality under the law but also in protest over the actions of the police. The numbers involved were large, as the GLBTQ communities were increasingly supported by other citizens and several civil liberties groups. The demonstrations in Adelaide, Melbourne, and Sydney involved more police interventions, more conflict, received broad radio and television coverage, and became a major embarrassment for the New South Wales government which had claimed to be a strong upholder of civil rights[40].

Now, two months after the original Mardi Gras Parade and demonstration, things were heating up yet again as the protesters learned that the government was debating whether to change the laws in favour of sexual equality. One more large protest might be enough to tip the scales, it was thought, and more than a thousand people had already turned out to begin a march, with more likely to join along the way. Their mood was still one of brooding anger.

As the march began, so did the chants. As the crowd passed downtown bars, the chants changed to "Come out of the bars and join the march!" Many people did. When they reached Hyde Park for the speeches, the police had barricaded it and denied them entry. When, on top of this, the police ordered the crowd to disperse, the brooding anger and pent-up energy of the crowd resolved themselves into a defiant, continued march through the streets of the city. The chants were resumed as well, beginning with one of the classic anthems of the civil rights movement, '*We Shall Overcome.*'

As the crowd continued to increase in numbers, so did the size of the police presence with seemingly endless streams of paddy wagons arriving on nearby streets. Among the police reinforcements was a man wearing the uniform of the New South Wales police force, but with no badge or identification number. It was the former Major Jones. Beyond the uniform, his only other elements of disguise were that his short hair had been dyed brown, and the addition of a false moustache of matching colour.

As evening set in, from the centre of one of the police lines, Jones closely watched both the demonstrators and police, waiting for the pivotal moment. Finally, it came. A particularly raucous burst of yelling and rock-throwing shifted the balance of pushing and pulling and several police officers waded into the crowd, swinging their batons with intent to injure. Major Jones waded in with them, yelling and swinging his baton even more violently than the others.

Many of the protesters fought back, of course, which soon led to numerous people falling or being pushed and the scene became one of chaos. As the riot, which was what the encounter had now become, escalated the confusion was compounded by the semi-darkness. Projectiles thrown by the demonstrators were now as likely to strike other demonstrators as they were the police. At this point, Major Jones took out his Deer Gun and, concealing it close to his body, shot the police officer immediately to his right.

"Over there! The shot came from over there!" he yelled, pointing towards his left.

As the nearby police officers surged to the left, more aggressively than ever before, Major Jones judged that it was time for him to fade away. As he began to do so, however, he was struck by a forceful blow to the back of one shoulder that drove him to his knees. Recognizing that remaining low to the ground made him vulnerable to worse injuries, he struggled to get back on his feet but a helping hand from a nearby police officer was countered by another demonstrator who hit him on the side of the head with a sizeable rock.

Dazed and lying on the ground now, he was alternately kicked and simply walked over by any number of people. In the darkness, it was hard to tell whether he was being trod upon by demonstrators or police officers. It didn't matter. All he knew was that he needed to get up, clear a space, and get away – but he couldn't.

He thought he was finished, when one of the largest policemen he'd ever seen in his life lifted him up with a single arm, hoisted him over his shoulder, and simply bulled his way out of the rioting chaos and towards the rear of what was left of the nearest police line. Once there he simply said "Stay quiet mate, and wait for the medicos to get around to you," and then plunged back into the rioting mass.

Major Jones forced himself to lurch to his feet and slowly limped off to the rear of the police line, and along the rows of paddy wagons. When he reached the last one in line, he got in, verified that the keys had been left in the ignition, started it up and put it into reverse. When there was enough space in front of him, he shifted it to forward gear, turned around and accelerated away, turning on its flashing blue lights as he did so.

That was too close, he thought to himself, *maybe I'm getting too old for this sort of thing*. It had been a bizarre job as well. He was used to being hired by shadowy forces on one side or the other of demonstrations but this time he'd been hired by a shell-company that he strongly suspected was working for one of the ultra-conservative organized religions. Being hired by the church to break multiple commandments was a new one for him.

Maybe just one more, he thought, as he continued to drive away along empty, dark streets. *Just that last job I agreed to do in Labrador and I'll finally retire.*

The abandoned paddy wagon was found the next day, near the dockyards. The discarded Deer Gun was found near the epicentre of the worst of the previous night's rioting, and was an unusual enough discovery that it was brought to the attention of the Australian Federal Police (AFP), who in turn contacted the FBI to see if it could be identified.

It was.

***

27 August 1978
Somewhere off the New England Coast, U.S.A.

Coincidentally, the same day that Major Jones waded into the gay rights demonstrations in Sydney Australia, some ten thousand miles away, Captain Mickey Webb was preparing his ship, the *MV Ocean Saviour*, for a dangerous manoeuver off the United States' New England coast.

It was nearing the end of the whaling season for North Atlantic Right Whales and, having been stymied all season long in his attempts to inhibit the illegal hunting of Right Whales, Webb was frustrated and out of patience. He'd resolved to 'make a difference' one way or another, and had decided to tackle the pirate whaler *Sierra* head-on – literally. A source in a Washington-based conservation organization had provided Webb with the Sierra's approximate location, and it had taken a few days patrolling to actually find it. *But they had found it,* Webb thought, with satisfaction.

As the *Sierra* completed a refueling and reprovisioning stop and left port, heading for the open sea, the *Ocean Saviour* was lying in wait. The skipper of the *Sierra* was probably not very concerned. They had tangled with the *Ocean Saviour* before, and were well used to its usual tactics of sending Zodiacs out to buzz around and make their hunting difficult. On this occasion, however, the bridge watch reported no Zodiacs being deployed, which was curious. Yet the ship kept on sailing directly towards them. *A game of chicken, perhaps,* the shipper of the Sierra thought to himself.

On the *Ocean Saviour,* Webb decided it was time. Soon, the skipper of the other ship would realize something was up and take evasive action.

"Full speed ahead. Steer for just before the bow," Webb ordered the helmsman, as he picked up a handset to call the various departments of his ship and warn them that a collision was imminent.

For his part, and as soon as the skipper of the other ship saw the
Ocean Saviour increase speed but not change course, he ordered his helmsman to increase speed and steer hard to starboard. As a result, the *Ocean Saviour*, which had been attempting to use its

reinforced bow to destroy the *Sierra's* harpoon gun, was only able to strike a glancing blow. The *Sierra* was forced to slow down and check for damage, however, which allowed Webb to bring the *Ocean Saviour* around and take another run at her.

The second ramming struck the *Sierra* amidships and left a sizeable hole in its hull. Secure in the knowledge that the *Sierra* would be out of commission for a long time, Webb left it to limp back towards the nearest port[41] while the *Ocean Saviour* headed for Fredericton, New Brunswick.

The surviving mother whales would now be able to continue their journey south, to the waters off Florida, to calve.

Captain Mickey Webb

> *"Anyone who makes his living from the torture, trauma, and death of animals is less than scum, should be squashed underfoot and then roasted, slowly and painfully, upon arriving in Hell."*
>
> An opponent of the seal hunt.

Captain Webb pulled the letter[42] from his typewriter, signed it with a purposefully indecipherable script. Folding the letter, he sealed it into a previously addressed and stamped envelope, then tossed it into his out-basket with the rest. *Another letter-to-the-editor to another newspaper, from another seal-hugger*, he thought, smiling grimly.

Done with whalers for a while, and having returned to the *Ocean Saviour*'s home port of Fredericton, Captain Webb had turned his attention to the annual seal hunt. He was in the middle of typing another copy of the form letter when a crew member knocked on his door.

"Someone here to see you, Captain."

"Arne Kristiansen from IAAP?"

"I think so. That's what he said his name was, anyway."

"Fine. Show him up would you please?"

"Arne!" he said, when his visitor was shown to his cabin, which also served as his office, "have a seat."

"How are you Mickey? Any luck with the whalers this time?"

"I'm fine, but we had so little success with those damn whalers that I lost my cool and deliberately rammed the pirate ship *Sierra* off the New England coast."

"Good for you," was the prompt reply. "Sunk her, I hope?"

"No, but we rammed her twice. Couldn't get to her harpoon gun, so on the second run we put a good-sized hole in her hull amidships. Left her limping for port when we last saw her. She's a dockyard job now – should be out of commission for next year too."

"Well done, Mickey. Are the police after you?"

"That's the funny thing. No one chased us out, and my sources tell me that no notices have been put out about us either. I think that's because it's a foreign-registered pirate with murky ownership. The Americans don't like ships that register in small Caribbean countries so they can pay low wages, avoid most fees, and ignore international regulations. One of my sources told me that, off the record, the port authorities are pleased with us, and that they're looking forward to finally getting some money out of her for dockage and repairs."

"Well I'll be dammed. Like I said, good for you…. Now then, what do we do about the seal hunt next year?"

"I'll tell you right off, Arne, that I'm frustrated with our lack of progress so far. The demonstrations aren't making enough of a difference. No matter what the quotas are, and no matter what our protesters do, the hunters still take about 160 thousand seals each season. Demonstrating in Ottawa, demonstrating in Newfoundland, demonstrating on the ice itself isn't doing it for us. Even last Spring, when we went out and sprayed the pups' fur with green dye, we didn't save very many seals because we couldn't spray enough of them before the sealers and the police arrived."

"I agree. So, I take it you want to try something different next year?"

"I do. We need something that will generate more media-coverage. Prime-time, coast-to-coast coverage, at a minimum. Overseas coverage if we can get it. We need to reach more people to have any chance of fueling a larger anti-sealing movement."

"How about using the *Ocean Saviour* to blockade the St. John's harbor for a couple of weeks to bottle-up the sealing ships[43]? The Narrows there is well named: it's narrow enough for a single ship to block."

"Maybe, but I'm not sure we'd get enough publicity out of it and I wouldn't put it past the Coast Guard to bring in police and tugs to push us out of the way. I still think we should try some kind of publicity stunt."

"Hmmm. Headline news… How about if we bring along a famous actor? A woman, preferably, that we could photograph cuddling a baby seal in a protective, motherly embrace. That sort of thing?"

"I like it. Can we afford it?"

"By 'we' I take it you mean the IAAP? You're usually lucky if you can pay your fuel and dockage costs, not to mention your crew… Wait a minute, let me think…. When that French actress, Brigitte Bardot came over a few years ago, it made big headlines in Europe. She was expensive though. Maybe if we could find another actress that is very well known, is a supporter of animal rights causes, but is still rising in her career. A combination of sympathy and the extra publicity it would bring for her might be enough to bring her fee down to something we could afford."

"Do you know anyone like that?" asked Mickey, getting interested now.

"Maybe, there are a couple of actresses I can think of. It would be even better – and cheaper - if we can find a well-known but rising Canadian actress. Hmmm… you ever watch *The Beachcombers* on TV when you're in port?"

"Sure. You're not thinking of the blonde?"

"That's right. Ginger Brandt. Former beauty contest winner, former Playboy model, one of the stars of *The Beachcombers*. Someone who's on her way up in Hollywood too from what I read. Best of all, she's a member of IAAP!" he concluded with a flourish.

"You're kidding."

"Not at all. Signed up last year, with a nice contribution, too. Turns out she's a supporter of Greenpeace and few other outfits as well, but her passion is animal rights."

"Can we get her?"

"I don't know, but if you agree I'll see what I can do. I'll call a few agents, put out some feelers, that sort of thing, just to keep our options open. But I'll make a special plea to Ginger Brandt's agent… wine-and-dine, the whole shebang."

"If you can get Ginger, the local media will fall all over themselves to cover us. Imagine if we can film her out on the ice hugging a whitecoat and holding off a horde of ugly, bloodthirsty sealers!"

"Now you're talking, Mickey. So, let's plan this whole thing out. We'll need a more detailed plan than usual if we're going to get a horde of media out in St. John's, and a decent sized group to commit to a few days at sea and on the ice with us when March comes around."

The planning went on for several hours, but when it was concluded they had the outline of a workable plan and schedule, and both men felt well satisfied that they'd have better success in the 1979 season.

Laurie Schramm

St. John's Harbour and the Narrows

6 CALM BEFORE THE STORM

January 8, 1979
Ottawa, ON

It was a Monday, one week after New Year's Day, when I received a call from Ginger.

"Happy New Year Alex, it's Ginger Brandt. Remember me?"

"Of course, I do. Happy New Year to you too."

"My agent got a call from the IAAP. They want me to join them in early March for a trip on the *Ocean Saviour*. There will be sealing protests and a documentary movie filmed. We said yes, and that I'll be bringing an assistant along with me."

"Great. Do you know where they're going?"

"Somewhere called 'The Front' off the coast of Labrador. Can you get to St. John's by March 9?"

"Sure."

"OK then. My assistant here will send you an itinerary, the same background information they'll be sending me, and we'll have a hotel room booked for you. Apparently, the ice conditions are good so far, and they're expecting the seal pups to be born sometime in the following two weeks. The plan is to stick around St. John's until they get word about the pups, then sail on the *Ocean Saviour* up to the ice pack and make a big fuss over the pups for the cameras. You and Silver will have your own cabin, right next to mine, same as at the hotel. OK?"

"Sounds good. We'll drive to North Sydney, Nova Scotia and take the ferry to Port aux Basques. That should get us there by mid-afternoon."

"Great. Keep your receipts. Everything's being paid for by IAAP and the Ocean Saviour Foundation. My assistant will also send you some contact names and phone numbers you can call if you have any questions or problems later. I'll be down in Hollywood filming a new movie, but either my assistant or my agent will be able to get messages to me. I'll be in St. John's by March the ninth."

"Thank you Ginger. We'll see you then!"

"OK. Got to run now. Bye!"

And that was that, we'd have another chance to spot the elusive ex-CIA guy… maybe… if he was even going to show up. *Oh, well, I thought, it should be a nice relaxing trip if nothing else.*

I was wrong, of course.

Other than letting my boss, Bob, and my boyfriend, Don, know what I was going to be getting up to next, my only other preliminary was to phone Vivian at her FBI office. I gave her the same information I'd received and told her that I would be posing as Ginger's assistant and bringing Silver along with me. She said she'd try to join our expedition as well and that she'd come up with something for a cover story.

As I told Ginger, I had planned to drive from Ottawa to Cape Breton Island, Nova Scotia and then take the ferry to Newfoundland from North Sydney. When I tried to make a ferry booking, however, I discovered that the ferry to Argentia, which is fairly close to St. John's, only runs from mid-June to late September. The other ferry option, to Port aux Basques, runs year-round but involves a 7-hour crossing followed by a 9-hour drive.

I decided we should fly, but since I wasn't willing to put Silver through the ordeal of travelling in the baggage hold, we'd have to travel officially so he'd be allowed into the passenger cabin with me. Although I wasn't going to travel in uniform, I'd have to identify the two of us to the airport authorities and the airline and hope that the other passengers simply assumed that he was accompanying me as a service dog. To further reduce the risk, I decided that we would fly out a few days early. That would also

give us a chance to walk around St. John's and maybe learn how the locals felt about the seal hunt.
March 7, 1979

When early March arrived, and we went to the airport, I identified Silver and myself to CP Air[44] at check-in. They took everything in stride – even my desire to be inconspicuous and let people assume that Silver was some kind of service dog – and they even moved me to a new seat that was beside an unoccupied one, so that Silver would have more room to lie on the floor. When we changed planes in Halifax for the flight to St. John's, they were one step ahead of us, and had given me another seat beside an empty one. The extra seating made a big difference, and the flight attendants made such a fuss over Silver with water and snacks that he radiated contentment. I told him that I thought he was being spoiled, even though I didn't expect him to understand the word spoiled but, as always, he correctly interpreted my thought and managed to look rather smug.

Knowing that I might need an easy way to get around St. John's, whether related to my mission or to running errands for Ginger, I picked up a rental vehicle at the airport – a 1980 Ford Bronco SUV[45]. This had lots of room for Silver and I, and we were soon driving into St. John's and following the long sloping turns that would take us downhill to the harbour. I'd booked a room at The Battery Hotel[46], which was located partway up the famous Signal Hill but still very close to the downtown core and the harbour-front. As we started up the hill, we soon came to the turnoff for the hotel grounds and passed between two vintage, cast-iron muzzle-loading cannons that were positioned like sentinels. I found out later than they had been recovered from a shipwreck in Placentia Bay, on Newfoundland's southeast coast.

Ginger's assistant had booked us a beautiful suite that had a fantastic view of the St. John's harbour and downtown core. Once we'd settled in, I was doubly glad that we'd arrived early as it would give me a chance to absorb some of the rich history of the area. We started this almost right away, as there was time for a walk before supper. For our first walk we did Signal Hill, which is a marvel on its own. From sea level, it rises some 167 metres (nearly 550 feet) and is capped by old fortifications and the famous Cabot Tower. Near the summit, the challenge is whether to focus on the rich history or the stunning, panoramic views. Naturally, I did both.

I learned that Signal Hill has been the pinnacle of St. John's harbour defences from the wars of the 17th century right through the First- and Second World Wars. Along the way, it was also the site at which Marconi received the world's first transatlantic wireless signal, sent by Morse Code in 1901.

At one of the many scenic viewpoints, Queen's Battery, nine large cannons, still mounted on their gun carriages, still crouched behind the fortifications from which they defended the harbour from enemy ships in the 18th and 19th centuries. I made a mental note to remember to tease Vivian, if she succeeded in joining me, with the fact that the last major modernization of the Queen's Battery cannons was in 1862, when the British sent additional troops and artillery to protect St. John's from the Union Navy.

The next day, Silver and I took a longish walk along the harbour-front docks, all the way from Battery Road, at the base of Signal Hill, past the downtown core to the containership pier at the south end[47]. After turning around to walk back, we strolled up a block to Water Street to get a cup of coffee for me and then headed back down to the docks to find a place to just sit and a look out at the inner harbour. I had worn a daypack with water and a bowl for Silver, and I was just pouring the water for him when a man came up and sat down beside us.

My clothes must have marked me as being 'from away[48]' because his first word was "Visiting?" as he filled and lighted a pipe.

"Yes, I'm from Ontario but I sure enjoy every chance I get to visit Newfoundland."

"Lived here all my life," he said, contentedly, and in between puffs from his pipe. "Been a fisherman since I was old enough to stand up and keep my balance in a boat."

"Do you still fish?" I asked.

"Yes b'y. My boats' right over there across the harbour."

"I think I read somewhere that the fishing fleets are taking in more fish each year. Is that right?"

"You're right there, but you have to look a bit deeper. The fish stocks used to be growing but now they've passed the peak and the numbers are decreasing each year."

I noticed that he had the Newfoundland habit of saying 'fish' when he specifically meant cod. Taking his pipe out of his mouth, he continued. "There's two things that have been going on. First," he waved his pipe stem in the air, "new technology lets us fish a bigger area, trawl deeper, and stay out on the water for longer at a time. But the new technology is a curse in disguise because it's given us the ability to take fish out faster than they can breed and get replenished.

"Second," he waved his pipe stem in the air again, "a few years ago – 1976 it was - the government moved the exclusive fishing zone out to 200 miles offshore. The idea was to fix the decreasing fish stocks by kicking the foreign fishing boats out."

"Didn't that help?" I asked.

"It looked like it at first, but then the government increased the quotas for Canadian and American trawlers so nothing really changed and the fish stock just keeps on dropping."

"Won't they reduce the cod quotas then?"

"Doesn't look like it. Seems like the politicians and bureaucrats are afraid to admit they made a mistake, so they keep arguing that the fish are there but we fishermen are too incompetent to find them. Hah! We spend our lives out there on the water. The fish stocks are dropping all right. That's why I'm against the seal hunt."

That caught my full attention. "What? The seal hunt? I thought everyone here supported the seal hunt."

"Well, it's just one more thing on top of the overfishing. See, the seals eat fish that eat baby fish."

"I don't understand."

"Sorry, there's fish and then there's fish. Let me try it again. The seals eat fish that eat baby cod. That's good for the fishery. But, if the seal population drops due to their being hunted, then there's more predatory fish available to eat the baby cod. One more thing taking the cod population down is one more thing we don't need – right?"

"I see. I guess I didn't think about the predator-prey relationships."

"There you go. Everything's connected, the fish – I mean cod – the other fish, the seals, even the plankton. That's why the government messes things up every time it steps in and makes a new regulation. It's because they only change one thing and don't take into account the way the whole system works. It's stupid, but they do it over and over again."

"What's the answer then?"

"Simple." Out came his pipe again to punctuate each point. "We fishermen have been fishing these waters for generations and the older the crab, the tougher its claws[49], as they say. We know all too well when the area is being overfished. The government needs to tackle the whole problem, not just the little pieces: keep the foreign fishing fleets out - the Americans included - reduce the fishing quotas, and restrict the seal hunt to the Inuit people that need it to survive. Then the fish will come back[50]."

We sat in companionable silence for the next while, enjoying the view, the weather, and the boat activity in the harbour. "Well, time for us to continue our walk," I said, eventually. "Nice talking to you."

"Fair weather to you[51]," was his reply.

Since we had another day free before Ginger's arrival, I decided we should spend it sightseeing. An easy drive took us through the downtown core and then overland until we reached Cape Spear, where two lighthouses perch at the edge of a rugged cliff that marks the most easterly point in North America. One of the lighthouses was built in 1836, and rises right up out of the roof of the lightkeeper's residence. No longer active, it was retired in 1955 when the second, more modern lighthouse was commissioned. The newer light house is of the familiar octagonal-tower-with-balcony design that can be seen in many other parts of Atlantic Canada.

Among the short walks at Cape Spear is a winding path that leads down and around the point to Fort Cape Spear, which still houses the twin, 10-inch guns that formed part of the St. John's harbour defenses during the Second World War.

I was standing on the edge of the fortifications, looking out at the open sea and enjoying the brisk wind and smell of ocean air, when I noticed another visitor stroll up beside us. It was an older but vigorous-looking man of about my own age who was also walking a dog and sightseeing. The typical reactions of our dogs, that had them cautiously circling and sniffing each other, prompted a brief conversation. A few light remarks led the conversation to how much we each enjoyed Canada's ocean coastlines, which happened to remind him of the TV series *The Beachcombers*.

"Did you know that Ginger Brandt, one of the stars is supposed to be coming here to help protest the seal hunt?"

"Yes, I read that in the paper this morning," I replied. "Are you a fan?"

"I'm a big fan! I watch the show every week. In fact, I'm planning to go see her arrival at the airport tomorrow, so I can see what she's like in person."

"Sounds interesting, but I don't like crowds very much."

We drifted on to other topics before I moved on, using the excuse of getting a bit chilled from the cold offshore wind. As we walked away, it occurred to me that he was about the age and build of our ex-CIA quarry, the elusive Major Jones, master of disguises. *Could that have been him?* I wondered, as a second chill struck me – one that had nothing to do with the weather. I decided that it was improbable, since Silver hadn't reacted to him at all, and decided that I was letting my imagination run away with me. *All the same*, I thought, it was a good reminder that we were hunting a dangerous killer and I would need to remain vigilant.

Ginger arrived the next day, and Silver and I did go to the airport to observe her arrival even though we didn't plan to meet until she was settled into the hotel.

Naturally, the media had been alerted in advance and they were there in force to greet her. As she entered the main terminal building, there was complete mayhem as a wave of reporters pressed forward, many of them yelling questions at her – so many, in fact, that it was almost impossible for me to understand what the questions were – and all amid a blaze of light from the television camera crews and the almost continuous flashes of brilliant light from still cameras.

It was interesting to see how well Ginger handled things. None of the lights, noise, crowd, or shouted questions seemed to faze her in the least. Stopping for only a moment to size-up the audience, she then quickly made her way to a baggage carousel and stepped up onto it so that everyone, including the cameras would have a good view of her. Then she held her hands up for the crowd to quiet down and waited patiently for the noise to subside, which it did, almost immediately.

"Thank you for coming to see me. I'll be happy to take questions," she said, "but one at a time please, so I can hear them." Then she pointed at one of the reporters in the crowd and said, "Let's start with you," and then she methodically worked the crowd, picking out reporter after reporter.

Was it true that she was there to protest against the seal hunt? "Of course," she said, "I abhor cruelty to animals, and this seal hunt is barbaric. They're planning to kill 200,000 poor, defenseless seals this year including baby seal pups! It's horrible and it needs to stop."

What was she hoping to achieve there? "I want the Canadian government to stop protecting and subsidizing the seal hunt and all other governments to prohibit all imports of sealskin."

Was she going to speak to the government directly? "I don't know. I hope so. I have asked for meetings with the Premier of Newfoundland and with the Prime Minister, but their offices always say they are too busy.... Too busy, can you believe it? How can they be too busy to talk about the torture and killing of defenseless animals, I'd like to know."

Not all the questions were as friendly and leading as these, but she handled them all with ease. For example, a reporter asked whether she wasn't simply out to gain publicity for her TV series and her upcoming new movie. "Look," she replied, "an actress needs all the publicity she can get, but when I'm out for publicity I go to the big cities like New York and Hollywood because I get more bang for the buck there. But when I come to Newfoundland, it's either for a cause or a vacation – because I love the people, and the ocean, and the beautiful scenery you have here. In this case, I'm here for a cause – the cause of the Harp Seals."

That was a pretty good reply, I thought, but it led to another difficult question. If she loves the people, she was asked, then what about the local communities that need the money from the seal hunts, especially when there is no other income outside of the fishing seasons?

Uh oh, I thought, *that's a tough one*. But I needn't have worried, she was ready for that one too.

"I understand that people need to work and earn money so they can look after themselves and their families," she replied, "but killing these poor defenseless seals for their skins is a barbarous practice that should have been retired long ago.

"If the Canadian government took the subsidies that they currently throw at the seal hunt, and instead put them into factories that can easily make perfectly good synthetic fur products, it would provide good, year-round jobs and money for people here in Newfoundland and Labrador. Locally produced synthetic fur products could be sold all over the world. I'd wear them myself, and I'm willing to volunteer right now to helping to promote them."

What about the fishermen who need work outside of the fishing season? "Ecotourism," she fired back. "This is one of the most beautiful places on earth. Marine ecotourism, including seal and whale watching, would be a great option for fishermen and their boats, and can bring in far more money than seal hunting."

Surprisingly, those last few answers turned the tide and the next few questions focused on smaller things like how long she planned to stay, whether she was going to tour around the province while she was there, Hollywood gossip, and so on. Sensing that the impromptu media scrum had peaked, she quickly switched gears, thanked everyone for coming out to see her, and promised that there would be other opportunities to ask questions in coming days.

With that, she jumped down from the baggage carousel, and strode through the terminal. Although several reporters followed her, shouting questions and snapping more pictures, I was able to get into her line of sight long enough for her to see me and wave. "See you at the hotel" she mouthed, just before reaching the curb outside and stepping into a waiting limousine that was strategically placed, bore a large sign with her name on it, and had its rear door already open for her. With another wave, she was gone.

Wow, I thought, *like a whirlwind*. But a whirlwind with purpose. She'd been in complete control the entire time. I was impressed.

Ginger had taken a morning flight from somewhere, and had arrived in St. John's shortly after lunchtime. I knew that we'd been booked adjacent suites, and I guessed that it wouldn't be long after Silver and I had returned to the hotel that I'd hear from her, so I wasn't surprised when there was a knock on the connecting door between our suites. I was however, completely taken aback by the woman standing in the doorway when I opened the door on my side.

"Elizabeth Peterson," said the woman as Silver padded up to her, gave her hand a lick and received an ear rub in return.

After a double-take, I got a grip on myself and said "Ginger?"

The answer came first in the form of a brilliant smile. I knew that smile.

"It is you! But what a transformation." The woman standing in front of me appeared to be two or three inches shorter than the Ginger I'd met in BC, had hazel-coloured eyes (previously blue), lustrous, medium-brown hair cut short, wore no makeup, and had glasses.

"What do you think?" she said, giving a bit of a pirouette as she strolled into the room.

"I'm amazed," I replied, truthfully, and then as my brain started processing again: "I take it this is your way of avoiding fans and the media when you need to?"

"That's right. I told you before I'm a very private person in real life, and the only way I can achieve balance is to be able to leave the movie-star world now and again and just be the real me in the real world."

"So, you made up your own character?"

"Not exactly. Ginger Brandt is my stage name; Elizabeth Peterson is my original name. As for my appearance, this is the real me. The only made-up part, is that the Elizabeth Peterson that you see before you often pretends to be Ginger Brandt's personal assistant. That way, people can see her going in and out of my room without giving it another thought.

"The Ginger Brandt you saw at the airport yesterday was wearing high heels, blue contact lenses, a blond wig, and full makeup."

"And your..." I pantomimed cupping my hands below my breasts.

"Oh yes. Another marvel of modern engineering. Ginger wears bras that enhance the appearance of her breasts, while Elizabeth wears bras that diminish their appearance."

"I'm amazed," I said, for the second time, "and so simple."

"Like magic, in fact. Any magician will tell you that all their illusions are simple once you know their secrets. Some time when we're not on this adventure, I'll come see you in Ottawa and we'll do the reverse for you."

She looked me over appraisingly, which made me feel quite self-conscious and even a bit nervous.   "You have fantastic red hair and green eyes," she said, "I'd add a wig of the same colour to give it more body and length, makeup to bring out your eyes... I bet you don't wear skirts or dresses, do you?"

"No, not really. Not for a very long time anyway."

"So, a long silky gown, high heels to show your legs off, a push-up bra to focus people's attention, and you'll be the talk of the town. What do you say?"

"I'd say I'm skeptical, but what the hell, let's give it a try some time."

"Do you have a boyfriend?"

"Yes. His name's Don, but I'm not sharing him!"

"That's OK, when I'm done with you, we'll knock his eyes out! By the way, you figured me out pretty quickly when I walked in here. What gave me away?"

"It wasn't anything you did, it was Silver. He walked right up to you like he knew you and licked your hand. That was my clue. He doesn't do that with strangers, but he picked up on two things you didn't change: your scent and the sound of your voice."

"Smart boy, Silver. Good for you," she said to him. To me, she added: "Feel like a walk? I need some fresh air and exercise after that flight."

"Sounds great. Have you ever been to St. John's before?"

"Only once or twice."

"Well, one of my favourite things to do here is just walk along the harbour-front. How about that?"

"Let's do it, and by the way, please call me Liz when you're with the real me, OK?"

"Deal."

Since we were both already dressed in casual clothes, all we needed to do was to grab light jackets and sun hats, and off we went. As we exited from my room, I noticed that there were a couple of photographers hovering in the hallway and keeping a close eye on the door to her suite. Of us, they took no notice whatsoever. Once we were alone in the elevator, with the door closed, she turned to me and said "See, safely anonymous."

Unbelieveable, I thought.

The three of us did essentially the same walk that Silver and I had done two days previously, the only difference being that it was an overcast, grey day. When we neared the southern end of the accessible part of the harbour-front, there were two tour boats tied up, each with advertising stands set up nearby. One of them was the *Scademia*[52], which was billed as being the last old-school-type, two-masted schooner to have been built in Newfoundland, the kind that used to sail around Newfoundland as a fishing boat in a previous era.

"Would you like to try a short boat tour Liz?" I asked. "I went out on the *Scademia* the last time I was in St. John's and really enjoyed it. They do a run through the harbour, go out through the Narrows into the open ocean, and then over to see Cape Spear, before coming back. It only takes about two hours, so depending on when the next sailing is, we could still be back in time for supper."

"Sounds great," she replied.

"The only thing is, I don't know whether they'll let me take Silver on board. Last time I was here, was before Silver and I had even met."

Walking up to the display booth for the *Scademia*, I was pleasantly surprised to recognize the man standing there as the Captain of the schooner the last time I'd been on it. I asked when the next sailing was and whether or not we could take Silver on board with us.

"We don't normally allow pets on board, which is a bit of a contradiction because you'll see my Newfoundland dog come on the trip with us, but there won't be many people coming along since we're so far ahead of tourist season. As long as he's on a leash, you're welcome to bring him along. Next trip leaves in 20 minutes."

Thanking him, I bought two tickets for Ginger and myself – he refused to charge me for Silver – and we continued our stroll to kill time before the sailing. When we returned to the boat 15 minutes later, we were welcomed by the sounds of traditional Newfoundland music being performed by two local musicians who were sitting in the stern, one playing an electric violin and the other an accordion.

As we handed over our tickets to a crew member, the Captain was on hand to tell her that we could bring Silver on board with us. When we did, he personally led us to the stern to meet his Newfoundland dog who, we were amused to learn, was named Ginger. After suitable circling and sniffing, the two dogs decided they liked each other and remained close together for the entire trip. They made an unusual pair as Silver is a large dog, over two feet tall at his shoulder and about 85 pounds, but Ginger the dog was in a class all her own at about the same height but (according to the Captain) 120 pounds!

The boat cruise, of course, was great. To the sounds of rousing, Celtic sea tunes, the schooner did a circuit of the harbour then took us past old gun batteries and through the Narrows – the only passage into and out of the harbour, bounded by steep rocky cliffs, and only about 60 m (200 ft) wide at its narrowest. The schooner, under the power of its twin 100-horsepower engines, had no trouble navigating the channel, but I wondered at the skill that would be required to navigate a container ship through or, in days long past, ships that had only their sails to propel them through.

As we entered the open ocean, the musicians took a break from their singing and playing to become bartenders. This was our cue to get a couple of traditional Screech[53]-and-Cokes as the schooner plowed through the waves, heading for Cape Spear. This gave us time to sit, enjoy the journey, and chat while Silver was companionably stretched out beside Ginger, the Newfoundland dog.

Besides the dogs, we pretty much had the open deck to ourselves as the small number of other sightseers had quickly made their way into one of the two glassed-in, heated cabins. It was 10 °C, quite warm for March, but others seemed to find it quite cold. In fact, I was surprised that Ginger seemed fine with the cold, and asked her about it.

"I was born in Calgary and spent a lot of time in the Rocky Mountains. When you go there, you have to be prepared for all kinds of weather, and in any season. I remember camping near the Columbia Icefields Parkway one year, and getting snowed on in the middle of summer! Anyway, you learn to adapt and I've always loved being outdoors, no matter the weather…. This is Liz talking, mind you," she laughed. "Ginger would be freezing to death and worrying that the wind would mess up her hair."

Since there were no other ears around, we traded growing-up stories while the schooner made its way slowly but surely towards Cape Spear.

We were far too early for either the iceberg-watching (April – June) or whale-watching (May – Sept.) seasons, but it was still a fun trip that provided a unique view of Cape Spear's two lighthouses and lower fortifications. Even just getting out on the open ocean was enough for me.

On our return, the Captain put on a traditional Screech-In Ceremony by telling a couple of probably-fictitious (but certainly amusing) stories in an exaggerated Newfoundland accent and using so many colloquialisms that it was impossible to understand at times. After the stories, he asked us "Is yer screechers?" He'd already coached us on the correct answer, so everyone was able to respond "Indeed I is, me old cock, and long may your big jib draw," the latter phrase meaning "may there always be wind in your sail," or "good luck." In the second part of the ritual, the crew passed out samples of smoked cod to try.

In the third part, we were invited to "kiss the cod." On shore, such ceremonies usually involved being handed a frozen cod to kiss. On the schooner, it was an actual stuffed cod (that is, a real cod - taxidermically 'mounted' - not a plush, toy cod). Lord knows how old it was, or how many people had previously kissed it but, unhygienic or not, the stuffed cod was passed around for each person to kiss.

In the fourth part of the ritual, they gave us each a small glass of Screech to drink. The Captain then explained that because each of us had spoken, eaten, kissed, and drunk something 'Newfoundland,' we were entitled to a small scroll that proclaimed us to be honourary Newfoundlanders.

After the *Scademia* docked and we disembarked, we strolled up from Harbour Drive to Water Street, then one more street higher to Duckworth where there were quite a few restaurants.

"What do you feel like eating?" asked Liz.

"Seafood. How about you?"

"Anything! I'm famished."

In the end, we found a nice little restaurant with an outside patio where dogs were allowed. 'On leash,' of course. I knew Silver wouldn't mind too much as long as he got 'people food.' The restaurant people hadn't been planning to serve outdoors (it being only 10°C after all), but the tables and chairs were all there and our server kindly said "Why not?" and took it all in stride.

When we'd been served a pair of glasses of Chardonnay, and a bowl of water for Silver, we looked at each other for a moment. "That was great Alex. I felt free. Thank you," said Liz, contentedly sipping her wine.

"I really enjoyed it too. The wind, and the ocean, and the live music. It felt exciting through the narrows, and I especially liked the wild feeling of being out on the open ocean.... Did you enjoy just being 'Liz' for a while?"

"I love my job and my work, but I can't tell you how wonderful it is to be just me for a few hours and to have been able to spend it with a friend – a new friend."

I raised my glass in acknowledgement: "Cheers."

She raised her glass in return and, with an absolutely straight face said "Long may your big jib draw."

We both giggled, and relaxed even more as she continued. "The *Ocean Saviour's* due to come in tomorrow, so plain old Elizabeth will have to go back to being Ginger the actress."

"Well, I like you both," I asserted, "and for tonight you can still be Liz."

"Deal," she agreed.

It was a little chilly out there on the deck after all, but we persevered and had a nice quiet dinner. All by ourselves.

The Daily News

Saturday, March 10, 1979

Ginger Brandt to Protest Sealing
Famous Actress Turns Activist

When we met in her suite for breakfast the next morning, Ginger was energized and well-pleased with the Saturday morning newspaper and the earlier radio coverage that she'd received. She had also received a message that the *Ocean Saviour* ship had come in overnight, and was tied up along the dock on the edge of downtown.

To avoid the media, Ginger, Silver, and I went aboard very early to meet the Captain. As we approached the ship, we stopped for a moment to look up and take it all in. I suppose it wasn't huge compared with some commercial ocean-going vessels, like tankers and container ships, but it certainly appeared large from the point of view of someone standing on the wharf beside it. The *MV Ocean Saviour* was nearly 200 feet in length and had a beam of more than 30 feet. It had the word 'RESCUE,' in bold eight-foot-tall red letters, stenciled on its side, and there was a small helicopter secured to a landing flatform near the stern.

The gangway wasn't roped off, so we went up and were met at the top by a crew member who introduced himself by saying "Everybody calls me 'Red.' I guess you can tell why," he said, looking pointedly at my own red hair.

I laughed and said, "Yes, but I try not to let anybody get away with it!"

Chuckling, he escorted us to the Captain's cabin.

When we got there, and were announced, the Captain bounded up from his desk to greet us. "Mickey Webb, glad to meet you. Please have a seat," he said to Ginger, waving towards his one good visitor chair and sparing only the briefest of glances at Silver and I before continuing. "I think you already know Arne Kristiansen, President of IAAP. He'll be coming out with us."

"Hi Ginger, said Kristiansen, who was sitting perched on the Captain's bunk. "Nice to meet you in person. Thank you for agreeing to join us." Silver and I only merited a glance from him as well. Clearly, we were to be treated as lowly 'staff.' That was OK, as I didn't want to attract attention anyway. Silver and I simply stood quietly by the cabin door and watched and listened.

It was interesting to watch, as the two men treated Ginger like visiting royalty while she, for her part, accepted their fawning as if it was an everyday occurrence – *which for her it probably was*, I reflected – and yet she somehow still managed to convey the sense of empty-headed, wide-eyed innocence of the *Beachcombers* character that had helped make her famous.

While they chatted, it gave me time to size-up the two men. Kristiansen, I had had previously seen as the Ottawa protest leader the previous July. Up close, he seemed even larger than he had before, and still had a shock of rather unruly-looking dark hair. In Ottawa, he'd been the man with the megaphone but his normal voice was quite booming in the confines of the Captain's cabin, as he talked about the sealers and the need to stop them, pounding with a meaty hand on the wooden sides of the Captain's bunk to emphasize his points. *Like a bull in a china shop*, I thought to myself. Even his normal speaking manner suggested latent violence.

In contrast, Captain Webb wasn't physically imposing, and his manner was friendly and easy-going. He was of medium height, with a medium build, thick, sandy-coloured hair that was just long enough to look unruly, and he had the stereotypical sailor's clear blue eyes. He didn't add much content to the discussion, seeming content to make small jokes here and there, as if to take the rough edges off of Kristiansen's rather harsh and angry assertions. *This one's all smiles*, I thought to myself, and yet I sensed an underlying character that I though was probably different entirely. Those eyes were very watchful and I suspected that they didn't miss much. I wondered whether his easy-going exterior masked a mind of intelligence and cunning. Whereas my new impression of Kristiansen was of someone that would impulsively come and challenge a person or situation directly, Captain Webb would be more strategic, develop a plan first, and come at his quarry by stealth. Both men would bear watching, I decided.

I was jolted out of these thoughts when Ginger deftly turned the conversation to lighter matters, beginning with asking about the ship. "It seems so very large," she said, with a shockingly wide-eyed, vapid expression that very nearly made me laugh out loud. As it was, I had to deflect my surprise into a pretend coughing fit that earned me dark looks from both men. Apparently 'staff' were to be seen but not heard.

It was the right approach to make to the Captain though, as he smiled even more brightly than before and sat up straighter in his chair.

"We were lucky to find it," he said proudly. "It's classified as a research and survey vessel and used to be used for marine meteorological and oceanographic research. That made it well suited for our purposes. We haven't had it long. It was purchased in 1978 by the Ocean Saviour Foundation, and the only real modifications we had to make were to strengthen the hull to make her more ice-worthy."

"So, it's like an ice-breaker?" Ginger almost gushed.

"Well, I don't think I'd go that far..." He paused, as if

judiciously considering the question. "We can ram our way through one- or two-season ice, but not the really thick multi-season ice like the Coast Guard icebreakers can."

"You must have an awful lot of responsibility, with so large a ship. How many people will there be?"

Ginger had clearly found the source of his pride – his ship and everything on it. If anything, his chest swelled out even further than it had before. "For this sailing, we'll have about 45. That includes the crew, staff and volunteers from the Ocean Saviour Foundation. And, of course, the media." He went on to describe something of what it took to run a ship of the *Ocean Saviour's* size, and the nature of the volunteers that would form the main body of the protest demonstration on the ice pack. That led, of course, to the plan for the trip.

"We'll need two more days for supplies and minor repairs. You might want to move your things onto the ship on Monday and sleep here that night. We'll be sailing at high tide the next day."

"How exciting," said Ginger, in a breathless kind of voice. "How long will it take us to get to where the seals are?"

The Captain sat back in his chair and shifted into a pontificating manner. "Well now, we have to wait for the birthing to be well underway – almost over, in fact. That's what the sealers will be waiting for too, because they particularly want to go after the white-coated seal pups...." He steepled the fingers of his two hands at this point, and went on in a professorial tone to explain that once we got to the 'Front,' the ice pack off the southeast Labrador coast, they'd use the ship's helicopter to scout for the main parts of the herd and watch for the seal pups.

As for the time to sail from St. John's to the Front, he first looked up at the ceiling for a moment, as if considering the question. Then he shrugged. "Well, it's over 300 nautical miles and we'll most likely be cruising at about 13 knots so we're looking at around 42 hours just to get into the right area." He leaned forward at this point, and adopted a concerned tone. "A lot depends on how rough the seas are, of course. We'll get there a bit sooner if we have calm water, later if it's rough. Have you ever sailed on a ship before?"

"Oh no," she exclaimed. "Only those little boats that you see on our TV show... and the car ferries, of course," she added as an afterthought.

"Well, if you see the ship's doctor when you come back aboard, he'll give you something to help with seasickness. It's better to take the medicine before you need it, than to wait until you're not feeling well."

"Oh, thank you for being so kind," Ginger gushed again. "I'm sure everything will be just fine with you looking after us!"

"All part of the service," purred the Captain, charmingly. "I'll have someone show you your cabins, so you'll know what to expect when you next come aboard." Lifting a telephone-style handset, he pushed a button and spoke briefly, then replaced it and got up. "It was a pleasure to meet you in person Miss Brandt, and I'm looking forward to having you with us for the trip."

"It was my pleasure, I'm sure, and please call me Ginger," she purred.

Kristiansen had also risen by this time and put his hand out to shake. "Thank you again for agreeing to come with us on this trip Ginger. Once the world media see our documentary and the pictures of you helping us saving the baby seals, we'll be a big step closer to shutting down this despicable seal hunt."

"I'm looking forward to it!" she said.

There was a knock on the door, which opened to show a rather weather-beaten, tough-looking man that I judged to be in his mid-fifties. "This is Sam Hynes," explained Captain Webb. "He'll be looking after you while you're with us. He's been with this ship since it was commissioned and knows it like the back of his hand. Anything you need, just ask Sam."

"How do you do Sam?' said Ginger, holding out her hand and giving him a dazzling smile.

"Just you follow me, ma'am," was all he said, before turning to head down the passageway. But I had seen the look in his eyes before he turned. In only five seconds, Ginger had already hooked another fan.

Sam led us to the Boat Deck, which was below the Bridge Deck (where the Captain's cabin was), and just above the Upper Deck (the main deck, which ran the full length of the ship – from bow to stern). On the Boat Deck, we'd been assigned two adjacent, 'outside' cabins that would have been originally designed to house research scientists. Each cabin contained a double berth (bunkbed), a closet with pull-out drawers, and a desk unit. The two cabins shared a head (bathroom). Since the head had two sliding interior doors, one leading to each of our cabins, our cabins were essentially interconnected. The cabins were not huge, but since each was designed for double occupancy, they weren't tiny either and they were fitted with decent-sized rectangular-porthole windows as well.

Sam also gave us a partial tour of the ship, which still retained many of its original nameplates, like "Officers' and Scientists' Saloon" (meaning dining room), "Officers' and Scientists' Lounge" (and bar), "Library and Conference Room," "Hospital," "Laundry," and so on. It seemed pretty nice for a former research/survey vessel, and even had a sauna on the Tween Deck (which, as the name suggests, was between the Upper Deck and the Lower Deck).

After thanking Sam and leaving the ship, I couldn't resist telling Ginger how amazed I was at her performance.

"What do you mean?" she asked, with an air of innocence.

"Hah!" I said, "I already know you well enough not to fall for that wide-eyed, 'dumb and innocent' act you seem to be able to turn on and off like a switch. But the two men went for your performance hook, line, and sinker. It was unbelievable. They were lapping it up like starving kittens at a fresh bowl of cream, while I was constantly struggling to stay quiet and keep a straight face."

Ginger giggled. "Well, I am an actress after all.... To be completely honest though, all I had to do was give them what they expected. They already thought of me as if I'm the character I play on TV, so all I had to do was play along and not disappoint them."

"I still think you're a wonder, Ginger."

She giggled again and took my arm. "You know, I'm going to enjoy having a friend along that also knows the real me."

"I'm looking forward to this trip myself," I admitted. "Just please try to remember that it won't be all fun and games. Don't forget, I'm after a killer, so while you're playing games with all the men as Ginger, please make sure your inner Liz stays sharp and keeps her wits about her."

"I promise," said Ginger, instantly sober, "but we still have the rest of today and all of tomorrow before things get complicated – right?"

"Right," I agreed. "What would you like to do next?"

"Let's trade," she suggested. "I'll pick something for this afternoon and you pick something for tomorrow afternoon, OK?"

"What about tomorrow morning?" my analytical mind wanted to know.

"Tomorrow morning, we sleep in," she said with a firm tone. "It might be our last chance for a few days."

"OK then, it's a deal," I said, laughing. "So, what do you pick for this afternoon?"

"How about a hike? The hotel's front desk gave me a brochure that describes some short hikes around Signal Hill. I thought we could do the North Head Trail and then the Ladies Lookout Trail."

"Those are great hikes, I did them the last time I was in St. John's. There's something irresistible about them. The views are fantastic."

So, that's what we did – with Ginger back in her 'Liz' persona. Having found a nice spot for an early lunch on the way back to the hotel, with an outside deck of course, we slipped back to our rooms to grab our raincoats – just in case – and some bottles of water, then went walking.

It was a fairly typical spring day in St. John's: partly cloudy, with a moderate onshore breeze. Since the Battery Hotel was itself partly up the side of Signal Hill, we had to first walk down to get to Battery Road, which led us through a small community known – appropriately enough – as The Battery. Although known as an artistic/fishing community, one's first impression is inescapably the kaleidoscopic collection of brightly-coloured homes. Our second impression was one of wonder, that the beginning of the North Head Trail was also the front deck of someone's house. Being big-city people, our first instinct was to conclude that we must have gotten our directions mixed up, because surely a public trail wouldn't cross someone's front deck – would it? But we were reassured by a two small signs, one proclaiming the deck to be the trailhead and the second, which simply said, "Public Entrance."

Tentatively, we mounted the stairs and crossed the deck, all the while feeling that we must be doing something wrong. "Only in Canada," said Liz, with a chuckle.

As we left the houses behind, the terrain became rougher and we found ourselves circumnavigating the steep-rock side of Signal Hill. As we did, we passed Second-World-War-era bunkers and a range of sights, from the sea and the Narrows below us, to a clear view along the length of the harbourfront behind and to one side, and a narrow path along the steep, rocky wall that lie ahead. In fact, portions of the path were so narrow and rough that some sections were provided with a heavy steel chain secured by eye-bolts that had been driven into the rock, while others were covered with wooden boardwalks and railings.

One of my favourite pictures of Liz is one that I took of her standing on the narrow path with both hands clinging onto the heavy chain, with the vertical, rocky face of the hill to one side and the open vista of the sea to the other. In the picture, she manages to look like she's timid and hanging-on for dear life, but in fact she took all of the hikes' challenges in stride, even when later we had to do some significant uphill stretches and, much later, when we had to contend with the final climb up a seemingly never-ending staircase up another almost vertical side of Signal Hill. It wasn't never-ending, of course, but it did have more than 1,000 stairs. Liz and I were both in pretty good physical condition, but we agreed that the 150 m (500 ft) ascent had earned Parks Canada's rating as "strenuous." Silver, for his part, seemed unfazed by the climb although even he seemed happy to have a few moments to rest and pant when we reached the top of the climb. He looked quite happy with his mouth open and his tongue drooping out to one side in a kind of wolfish smile.

Once we'd caught our breath, it was still only mid-afternoon, so we continued on to the trailhead for the Ladies' Lookout Trail, which wasn't far away.

The Ladies' Lookout Trail basically sticks to the 'backbone' of Signal Hill and, while it only has a modest elevation gain on its way to the summit, it is a much more rugged route than our previous hike had been. It had scenery though!

"Beautiful!" Liz would stop and exclaim every once in a while, as we reached yet another ocean vista. We'd been fortunate to pick a day that was neither rainy nor foggy, so the blue-grey ocean seemed to stretch out forever, until it was lost in the thin line that marked the horizon. Other than a few clouds and seabirds, it was all rock and ocean.

The summit, of course, was the "Ladies' Lookout" from which the trail gets its name. Our trail brochure explained that, in days past, women would go there in hopes of a first sighting of returning ships carrying their "husbands and lovers."

"I wonder how often their husbands and their lovers were travelling on the same ship?" said the irreverent Liz.

It was distinctly windy and chilly at the summit, so it wasn't very long before we decided it was time to head back. By the time we'd made our way down Signal Hill to our hotel, we'd been walking and sightseeing for nearly three hours.

The next day was Monday, our last day of freedom before joining the ship. It was my turn to pick an activity, and I chose another personal favourite.

"There's a group of small islands that are protected as a bird sanctuary near a fishing village called Bay Bulls. It doesn't sound like much, but it's a nice boat ride out and you have to see the birds and the islands to believe them."

"Sounds great! Let's do it," exclaimed Liz.

"OK. Bay Bulls is south of here, about half an hour's drive along the coast. Since we're not in the tourist season, we'll have to check around and see if we can persuade one of the tour boat operators to take us out. If that doesn't work, we might be able to hire a fisherman to take us out."

"Let's try it," said Liz. "I have a feeling we'll be lucky today."

So, we piled into my rental SUV about mid-morning and made the drive to Bay Bulls. When we got there, we parked and strolled down to the docks where quite a few tour- and fishing boats were tied up. Several of them sported signs of human activity, mostly people cleaning, repairing, or even painting parts of their precious boats.

Even though there were no signs or pictures painted on it, one of the boats looked like the kind that did fishing and whale-watching charters. It was a Cape Islander[54], probably about 40 feet in length, and instead of being full of fishing gear it had an open stern fitted with benches, a generous main cabin behind the wheelhouse, and there was an additional viewing deck on the roof of the main cabin. There was a man working on something in the boat's stern section, so that's where we headed first.

After saying 'good morning' to him, we explained that we were hoping to charter a boat to take us out to see the bird sanctuary at Gull Island[55]. "I took one of the tours there when I was last here, a few years ago. My friend hasn't seen much of Newfoundland, and I thought she should see more of it."

"Well," he said, scratching his chin thoughtfully, "you're a bit early. We're not into the main season yet, and the birds won't all be there."

Seeing out disappointed looks, he continued on a bit more encouragingly. "Don't get me wrong, now. The birds have been flying in pretty steadily the past few weeks, but there's more on the way that will be arriving over the next couple of weeks. I can take you out if you want – I just don't want you to be disappointed."

"We'll be fine," I assured him. "Even just getting out on the water and touring around a bit will be good for me." Liz nodded her agreement.

He smiled. "I think we can do better than that.… Now then, I'd have to charge you more than the tourist season rate to take just the two of you out. This old boat of mine eats fuel like you wouldn't believe."

"Can Silver come with us too?" I asked, pointing to Silver. "He's used to being on boats."

"Sure can, I only meant that I wouldn't charge for him."

"How much would it be?" asked Liz. This was a very different persona from the Ginger that had been on the *Ocean Saviour* the previous day. As Liz, she sounded like a businesswoman preparing to negotiate.

"The normal rate would be $45 per person, but with just two passengers – plus your dog – I'd need to charge you double that."

"So, $90 each then," said Liz. He nodded.

At this point Liz unleashed one of Ginger's trade-mark, brilliant smiles and said "OK then, I'll tell you what. How about if we pay you $200 and you throw in some sandwiches and something to drink. I'm starving!"

"No, no," he replied. "You're both visitors here, and I'm not going to let you get cheated. I'll take the $180, only, and if you'll give me a few minutes I'll go get my son and we'll pack some food and drink to bring along. OK?"

"There's just no negotiating with you is there?" This, accompanied by another brilliant smile. "My name's Liz, my friend here is Alex, and you've already met her dog Silver."

"My name's George O'Dell," he said, climbing up out of the boat, onto the dock, and holding his hand out to shake. "My house is just by the shore over there. Why don't you wander around the village here a bit and you'll see us when my son Jimmy and I come back to the boat."

We readily agreed, went for a stroll around the village, then made our way back to the docks and prowled them – looking at all the different boats that were tied up there. In what seemed like no time at all, we spotted George walking towards us, accompanied by a tall, gangling teenager who turned out to be Jimmy, his son. Soon, we were established in the stern of the boat while the O'Dells piloted us out of their small, well-protected bay and onto the open ocean. Before long, we were far from shore and cruising towards our destination. The wind was up a bit, and the sea was choppy, but being down low and behind the main cabin gave us some partial protection.

After taking in the scenery for a while, Jimmy came to let us know that lunch was available in the main cabin, where we found comfortable bench seats and two tables. Lunch turned out to be sandwiches and whatever we wanted from the bar, plus bowls of smoked fish (i.e., cod) and water. Silver particularly liked the smoked cod.

While we were eating, we noticed that an animated discussion, in hushed tones, seemed to be underway between the skipper, who was standing at the helm, and his son.

Uh oh, I thought. But I needn't have been concerned. Eventually, the skipper came back to where we were sitting and said, "Excuse me. Sorry to interrupt, but my son insists that you're Ginger Brandt from *The Beachcombers*, but he's too shy to come and ask you himself."

"Guilty as charged," replied Liz, reverting back to her Ginger persona and waving Jimmy over with a smile.

In between bites of her sandwich, Ginger fielded questions from Jimmy, who stood near our table, and George, who had resumed his position at the wheel.

Jimmy's first question was "Aren't you going to get sick, like you always do on the boats in *The Beachcombers*?"

"...and like you told Captain Webb," I murmured, *sotto voce*.

"No," she laughed. "In real life, I love the ocean and I only get seasick when it's really rough."

"You'll be fine today then," he said, knowledgeably. "It shouldn.t get any worse today than it is right now. It might even ease up a bit after we've gone round the islands."

After a few more questions, it was inevitable that they'd ask for a picture with her. She graciously agreed, which led to Ginger, George, and Jimmy crowding into the wheelhouse, with Ginger at the wheel, all of them smiling back at me in the main cabin, where

I'd been given the job of photographer.

"There you go," she said, after I'd taken several shots. "I hope one of them turns out for you."

"Can we put a copy up on the wall inside the main cabin?" asked George, hopefully. "It would help promote our business!"

"Put them up wherever you like," she said, "and if you send me a print, I'll autograph it for you and ship it back. Here, let me write out my address in Gibson's. If it arrives when we're not there filming, someone will forward it to me."

Well, she was their heroine for the day after that.

The bird sanctuary islands themselves were not huge, but they did rise impressively – and almost vertically – out of the sea. As we approached Gull Island, we moved up to the viewing deck that was the roof of the main cabin. Nearing the island, we could eventually see that what at first appeared to be roughness in the steep, rock faces was actually thousands and thousands of bird nests in every imaginable nook and cranny, and forming tier, after tier, after tier of nests. Even without the full complement of birds having arrived yet it was stunningly impressive.

"Like an apartment building for birds," I mused, "and they're all out sitting on their balconies."

"This is the spring home for the largest Atlantic Puffin colony in North America," explained George, who had slowed the engine and taken us in quite close so we could see the birds coming and going from their nests. With the engine noise much reduced, he was able to lean out of the wheelhouse door, point out the sights, and explain them to us. "In a few weeks, there'll be half a million puffins here."

As we made appreciative noises, George explained that Atlantic Puffins mostly live at sea, and that their parrot-like beaks only get their characteristically bright colours in mating season. "Quick! Watch right there," he exclaimed, pointing to a spot on the rock face where a puffin had wobbled to the very edge of one of the tiers.

No sooner had we identified the bird he meant, than it threw itself off of its perch and plummeted straight down towards the sea, with its stubby wings flapping for all they were worth. As Ginger gasped, it curved out of its fall at the last minute, barely avoided getting dunked, and flew off, skimming just above the waves, with its little wings flapping madly and occasionally even touching the water – sending up small splashes.

"My God," exclaimed Ginger. "I thought it was going to drown, and look how it's barely able to stay out of the water as it flies away even now.... Do they do that all the time?"

"Oh yes," said George. "He's gone off to hunt for small fish. If you keep watching, you'll see that they can actually kind of swim using their wing motions to paddle and their webbed-feet to steer."

Although we were fascinated by the antics of Newfoundland and Labrador's official bird, the islands provided nesting sites to more than just puffins. As we continued to slowly circumnavigate the four islands, George handed us each a set of binoculars and pointed out many other species of bird, including the one that outnumbered even the puffins. "Leach's Storm-Petrel," he said, pointing out several nearby examples of the smallish dark birds with white stripes running across their wings and tails. Whereas the puffins would occasionally dive underwater to fish, the petrels would grab plankton from the surface.

Each island was similarly congested with birds already, making it difficult to imagine what it would be like when all of the birds had returned to nest. "All told, there'll be upwards of 4 million birds here by next month," George said. "It'll be like permanent 'rush-hour' during the daytime, when they're all here."

When at last we had to say goodbye to the birds and head back to Bay Bulls, George offered to do a Screech-In Ceremony with us, but we explained that we'd done one just two days earlier.

"We'll take the Screeches though, if you're offering," said the irrepressible Ginger, and as we took our drinks onto the lower, stern deck to get out of the wind, George put some traditional Newfoundland music on the sound system.

All the way back to port Ginger and I sat back, enjoying the ocean, the rugged coastline, the Celtic-influenced seafaring music as we chatted away. It was heavenly, and it was only when we were in sight of the harbour entrance at Bay Bulls that we were brought back down to earth in remembrance of the next trip we'd be taking.

As we thanked George and Jimmy for our wonderful trip, Ginger reminded them to send a print of the picture I'd taken, so she could sign it, and insisted on paying for the whole excursion herself.

Laurie Schramm

7 THE CALL OF THE NORTH ATLANTIC

March 12, 1979
The *Ocean Saviour*

It was time to board the *Ocean Saviour*, which we did fairly early in the morning. Ginger and I were both interested in meeting our fellow voyagers, Ginger because she was excited about the adventure and the cause itself, and me because I hoped Silver would be able to help me identify the mysterious Major Jones.

At various times during the day, media people boarded the ship. These turned out to be of two types. There was the documentary film maker and his cameraman, who turned out to be from the BBC. The rest were reporter/writers from different print media. A woman from the IAAP was there to write media releases, and also to write a story for their quarterly newsletter to supporters and other stakeholders. Another woman was a reporter doing a feature story for *Macleans* magazine. One man was a freelance journalist, and another was a reporter from CBC's St. John's office. Finally, and one of the last to board the ship, was a reporter for *The New Yorker*, Vivian Rule.

The one thing all of these people had in common was that they all wanted to have an exclusive interview with Ginger. To each such request, Ginger would breathlessly exclaim that she would be happy to give them an exclusive and then airily say, "Just arrange something with my assistant." In other words, me. I say that as if it were a complaint, but I didn't really mind as it cemented my cover story and it also gave me a chance to meet and get initial impressions of each of them.

The interview with the BBC people was arranged for that very afternoon, in the Library and Conference Room. It was a good setting for a filmed interview. I noticed that when Ginger entered, she instinctively sized up the room and went directly to a chair at one end of the conference table where she would have a row of glass-fronted bookcases behind her, and a large window forward and to one side of her. This provided excellent lighting and a professional looking backdrop. The cameraman, meanwhile was able to set up his camera at a suitable distance away, from which he could pan and zoom as needed. As she took her seat, she immediately breathed, "Do you think this would be all right?" as if it were the purest accident that she had selected to best location in the room.

I was fascinated to be the fly on the wall, observing the whole process by which she remained in control of the entire interview while at the same time allowing the male interviewer and camera operator to feel like they were in charge. I will admit that I can sometimes be a bit devious myself, but here I was in the presence of greatness.

The interviewer began with some soft questions about her personal causes, which allowed her to explain the various animal rights causes and organizations she'd been supporting.

"Oh! I just can't abide cruelty to animals of any kind…. Can you?" she began, and then went into a lengthy answer.

Next, the questions shifted to the seal hunts in particular.

"Well," she explained, "this is another horrible example of humans being cruel. Every year, the hunters come here and go out on the ice to kill as many baby seals as they can. The poor little creatures are so trusting that they just lie there while the cruel hunters beat them to death and then skin them for their pelts." Already, at this point, there were tears in her eyes. "These hunts have been condemned all around the world, and they have to be stopped."

"What about this trip in particular?" the interviewer asked.

"I was asked by the IAAP to come along and observe the seal hunt and IAAP's protest of the killings, especially those of the poor little baby seals… and I am happy to be able to come along."

After this, the questions got a bit tougher. "Some people say that killing the seals is no different than killing cows, and pigs, and chicken. How would you respond to that? You do eat meat, don't you?"

"Of course I eat meat, but that is to survive. But the skins of baby seals don't keep anyone alive. Their pelts aren't even needed to make coats and jackets warm. They're only used to make clothes look fashionable." She sniffed, at this point, as if to imply that fashion was a poor excuse for wearing or doing anything.

"You realize that it's your famous name that they really want?" the interviewer continued.

"Oh! Do you really think so? How nice!" She paused for effect. "Well, if it helps with the cause, then that's OK isn't it, because sometimes it's hard to get people's attention when you want to talk about serious things, don't you think?"

The interviewer was forced to agree that yes, he thought that was probably the case, but undeterred, he went on. "What would you say to the people that say you're only here because of the publicity that you will get out of this? I mean all this media attention will be good for your career too, won't it?"

Ouch, I thought, but Ginger was ready for this too.

"Oh! I think that's so mean," she said, with a frown. "I think that if people want to check, they'll see that I've been supporting animal rights as much as I can for years now. My favourite charity is the SPCA, but as I told you before, I've done things with the Save-the-Whales people, and I've worked with IAAP before to try to save the seals."

"Well, what about money then? You must be getting paid a lot of money to come on this trip. What are people going to think about that?"

Just for a second, I thought I saw her eyes flash. *There's steel in there*, I thought. She only hesitated for that one second, though.

"Oh, do you really think they would have paid for me to come?" she asked, and then made another dramatic pause. "They didn't offer to pay me, except my travel expenses of course. It's very nice to think that they would have been willing to pay for me to come." Gushing again now. "I thought that only famous people got paid to do things like this."

"But Ginger, you are famous. That's why we're all lining up to interview you, and when the pictures and films of you trying to save the seals get broadcast, they'll go all around the world and part of the reason will be because of you."

"Oh, so you're so nice." Eyes very wide open now. "That's such a nice thing to say to me…. Well, all I can say is that if having little Ginger Brandt along helps gets the message out about the horrible things being done here, then I'll be able to die happy knowing that I did at least one good thing in my life."

The interviewer surrendered at this point, and moved to gentler topics, a few of which seemed to be aimed at producing comments from Ginger that could later be laid over filming that would be done out at the hunt itself and the accompanying protest.

The interview with the other two men, the freelance journalist and the CBC reporter went similarly, but not on such a grand scale. The two men certainly seemed like fans but not quite as susceptible to either Ginger's performance or the protest venture itself. *Just another assignment for them*, I thought to myself. They went through the routine, but I had the impression that's all it was – routine. Their lack of enthusiasm did make me wonder whether they were really reporters, but neither matched the appearance of Major Jones and neither produced any kind of reaction in Silver.

We came to a halt after the third interview, having scheduled the interviews with the three women reporters for the next day.

"What did you think?" asked Ginger, when we were back in her cabin, alone.

"I'm impressed," I said, frankly. "I didn't realize how demanding interviews would be, or how you always have to be ready for a penetrating question to leap out at you after a few easy ones. But you had them eating out of your hands the whole time. The tough questions didn't throw you off topic one little bit, and I think they went out believing that you have a heart of gold but are dumb as a post."

"What do you mean?" she asked, sounding perfectly innocent.

"You don't fool me. How about when he asked you a very simple question and you said 'What's that?' and put on the most vacuous, wide-eyed expression I've ever seen in my life?"

"I did not," she retorted.

"You did too!" I replied, just as strongly, "and it was so amazing, it threw them off completely."

"Yes, I did, didn't I?" she laughed, which got us both laughing. "Well, no one said I couldn't have fun on this trip, and besides, it's important to maintain the illusion of my character. It's also good practice."

With a bit of time to kill before supper, I looked in on the group of protesters that had boarded. This was mostly a younger crowd – a party crowd. Many seemed to be in their late teens and early twenties. They were easy to find, as they had almost immediately commandeered the Officers' and Scientists' Lounge, and I strongly suspected that the rock and roll music, which was already turned up loud and echoing down the steel passageways, would be a fixture for the duration of the voyage.

It was far too noisy in there to do more than look around, smile, and wave so I made a mental note to try to approach some of them individually when the ship was underway.

Our first shipboard supper was memorable, as the cooks welcomed everyone onboard with local favourites. The appetizers were cod tongue, which I didn't care for, and cod cheeks, which I loved. The main course was Jiggs' Dinner with Figgy Duff. The former is common throughout Atlantic Canada, and is a boiled dish made with salted meat (usually beef, or pork, or turkey), vegetables, and cabbage.

I'd never heard of Figgy Duff before. It is a bag-pudding dish, served for dessert. The name is misleading, as it contains raisins rather than figs, figgy being an old Cornish word for raisin. Filled, as it was, with molasses, brown sugar, and butter, it made for a tasty and hearty finish that seemed very appropriate on a ship about to venture into the North-Atlantic Ocean.

Over dinner, Vivian (in her guise as a reporter-at-large for *The New Yorker*) asked whether she could meet with me to get some background prior to her interview with Ginger, which was scheduled for the following day, and we agreed to meet in the Library and Conference Room.

"Well, here we are. Together again," said Vivian, closing the door and taking a seat. "how are you liking your role as personal assistant to a movie star?"

"So far, so good," I replied. "In real life, she's actually very nice. Intelligent too. That dumb and shallow act of hers is just that, an act. How about you? Any news on our elusive Major Jones?"

"Nothing recent. We did hear a strange story through

INTERPOL though. Apparently, he was involved in a gay-rights protest, that turned into a riot, in Sydney, Australia last August. The New South Wales police discovered another of the Deer Guns at the scene where one of their officers was shot and killed. The way they've reconstructed events, they think Jones must have been dressed as one of their own officers. He even stole one of their paddy wagons to make his getaway."

"Wow. Is that the first time he's killed someone?"

"Maybe. We really don't know. The Australian police are understandably mad as hornets, to the point of applying diplomatic pressure for us to find him and get him out of circulation. They're basically saying that a CIA Officer gone rogue is a U.S. problem, and that we should fix it, pronto."

"Ouch. I guess they have a point, though."

"They do.... One more thing. Apparently, he was beaten-up pretty badly in the riot. That's according to an officer that rescued him from the crowd."

"Badly enough to put him out of action?"

"No one knows. Maybe he's incapacitated, maybe a few serious injuries were enough to persuade him to retire? Who knows? I somehow doubt it though. I take it that you and Silver haven't spotted him either?"

"No." I told her about there being no signs of him at the Darlington Nuclear Station protest the previous July, and that we hadn't seen or sensed any sign of him on the *Ocean Saviour*. "Not yet anyway," I concluded, "do you think we're on another wild goose chase?"

"Could be, but we always knew we would just be playing the odds to come along on this trip." Vivian paused in thought. "My father was in the Marines and he used to repeat that old military phrase, 'They also serve, who only stand and wait[56]' I guess that's all we can do – wait and see."

"And be vigilant."

"Very vigilant. He's a trained killer. If he's around, he's dangerous."

"Well, I'm glad you're here."

"Likewise."

The next day was to be sailing day, but not until just before high tide, which was going to be at 7:39 pm. In the morning, while the ship's crew were busy loading the last of the supplies and running around making sure everything else was ready, Ginger did the remaining interviews. Once again, she was convincing and handled all of the reporters' questions with style and ease.

The last of them was Vivian. I had agreed not to expose Vivian's true identity, not because we didn't feel Ginger was trustworthy but because we didn't want to risk a chance comment or even a manner that might suggest Ginger and Vivian knew each other.

As far as the interview went, I thought Vivian did a convincing job as a reporter. She had obviously done her homework and asked a range of good questions about Ginger, her work, and her interests in animal rights.

When we finally left dock in the evening, there was a beautiful full moon. It seemed like a good omen.

For me, the highlight was sailing out of the harbour and through the Narrows. We had a great view from the Monkey Island deck, which was a small deck immediately above the Navigation Bridge, and which held the ship's searchlights, the main standard magnetic compass, among other things. It was a great vantage point for sightseeing and I couldn't believe how close the ship had to sail to the channel markers on each side, even at high tide. As we went through, the steep cliffside of Signal Hill loomed over us on the portside, while to the right we had a great view of Fort Amherst and its lighthouse and Second World War battery and fortifications.

After that, it was the open sea and the ship began to move around a bit more as the wind and swell increased.

"Sensible hat," remarked a passing crew member. I was wearing a bright reddish-orange, navy-divers-style toque of the kind that was popular among SCUBA divers at the time[57]. Whereas most Canadians refer to such hats as toques, people in Newfoundland (and Nunavut) often refer to them as simply hats. Ginger thought my toque funny, and to this day she still teases me about it.

Eventually, there was just the roll of the ship, reflections of light from the full moon, and little specks of light from lighthouses and the occasional other boat or ship. When the cold wind got us shivering, we abandoned the open deck for the warmth of our cabins.

Fort Amherst

That first night out, the sea became considerably rougher. Although the ship was stable in the rough water, it was not a gentle ride. Captain Webb explained that the originally fitted external stabilizers had been removed when the ship was modified to enhance its ice-breaking capabilities. Although he was reassuring, as the evening wore on the ship rocked more and more, occasionally violently, which didn't help any of us landlubbers get a good night's sleep.

The next day was to be a full day at sea, although there were not many early risers. This was partly because most of the passengers hadn't had a very sound sleep on their first night at sea. I hadn't had a great night myself, but I was an early riser by nature and one of the few that showed up for breakfast. Even so, the cook remarked that "the ones that are up are all crooked," a term some Newfoundlanders use for what the rest of us would call cranky.

After breakfast, Silver and I went up on deck again to look out at the rolling sea. It was quite chilly, especially with the sea breeze, so I had my red toque on again. This produced some interesting reactions. The ship's crew was comprised of several nationalities, mostly British and Canadian, with some Norwegians, Swedes, Americans, and Australians. My toque was a hit with the Scandinavians and Australians, wasn't even worth comment from the Canadians, and was a source of amusement to the Americans.

At lunch, as was the case with all of our meals on the ship, Ginger was very gracious about accommodating people's natural desire to want to sit with us at meals. As a result, we got to know quite a few of the people onboard through our mealtime conversations, and it allowed me to cement my role as Ginger's assistant. I was somewhat surprised to note how many people jumped to the conclusion that Silver was along as a kind of canine security guard for Ginger, which seemed to further deflect attention away from me, an added bonus.

That afternoon, Ginger did some further interviews with the various journalists, but for the most part everyone was waiting for the adventure to come, out on the icepack. As a result, we had most of the afternoon to ourselves.

I did manage to find a few minutes alone with Vivian, out on one of the open decks, and away from other ears, but we too had only a few bits of news to share.

We already knew that there were American warrants out for Jones' arrest. I told Vivian that there was now a Canadian warrant out as a result of the Toronto shooting. Vivian explained that the FBI had learned that Jones had spent some of the previous six months causing trouble in Europe, where his signature guns were found in the aftermath of violent political demonstrations in a number of East-European countries. Each of these exacted a heavy toll of injuries and deaths among both police and demonstrators.

Vivian added that there was also an Australian warrant for impersonating a police officer and for murdering a police officer. Her final bit of news was that at the request of the U.S., Australia, and Canada, INTERPOL had issued a Red Notice[58] concerning Jones.

Supper provided a welcome change of pace. This time, with everyone on board fairly well acquainted with each other, the dinnertime discussions were warmer and the topics more varied.

In the evening, Silver and I walked every deck and passageway we could find, partly for exercise and partly keeping an eye on things, but our walks were uneventful as well. Like most of the passengers, we turned-in early, in hopes of catching up on some the sleep we'd lost the night before.

The next morning brought us our second full day at sea. There were more early risers at breakfast, and everyone seemed to be in better spirits and eagerly anticipating the first sight of the icepack. It took much of the day but eventually, as if following the Captain's initial estimate, there was an announcement on the ship's loudspeakers at 2 pm – some forty-two and a half hours since leaving St. John's. "Welcome to The Front ladies and gentlemen!" crackled a metallic version of the Captain's voice.

When Ginger and I hurried to up the Monkey Island deck, we couldn't see anything but waves, with their white foamy tips as they crested and broke over and over again. Fortunately, a thoughtful crew member arrived with a pair of binoculars for us to use. When it was my turn to look through them it took some practice to keep the horizon in view against the rolling of the ship but when I finally got the hang of it, I could just make out a thin ridge of ice between the ocean and sky.

The next thing we heard was the sound of the helicopter's engine starting, followed by the sweeping sounds of the rotors as they began to turn and then spin faster and faster. Although the ship's helicopter was small, it was noisy when heard up-close, and it was soon too noisy for us to talk. We all knew that the helicopter was heading off to search for the seals, and especially to see whether large clusters of seal pups had been whelped yet. This created a heightened sense of anticipation among everyone on board.

It was nearly supper time when the helicopter returned, but the first order of business was to cram into the library for a briefing from the pilot and the spotter that had accompanied him. It was good news. Captain Webb and Arne Kristiansen had timed the voyage well, as lots of seals and pups had been observed on the ice, in several large clusters. Basically, the plan was to go the edge of the ice pack in the morning, and try to get the bulk of the documentary movie filming and picture taking done before the sealers arrived.

"Are the sealers close?" Someone asked.

"There was no sign of them from the air," replied the spotter.

"Maybe not, but they can't be far away," said Captain Webb. "We've been listening to them on the VHF radio. The fleet is out, and they're probably no more than half a day's sailing behind us. We'll use the helicopter to get a fix on them in the morning."

***

Earlier that same day.

In the wheelhouse of the fishing boat *Jonah's Escape*, Major Jones rested his coffee mug on the narrow shelf that ran along the lower length of the glass windscreen. Lifting a pair of binoculars to his eyes, he adjusted the focus and resumed his lookout. "There's no sign of the protesters and no sign of the icepack. Nothing but water," he said to the boat's skipper.

The skipper picked up his own pair of binoculars and took a long look in the indicated direction. "You're an impatient man, I see. They're probably half a day ahead of us, maybe more," he grunted. "I suppose this is as good a time as any to find out whether the police are on their way to help us or not."

"You don't know?" asked Jones, surprised.

"I don't know a damn thing. We knew the protesters would be going out to the Front. We complained to the police that they'd be trying to disrupt the hunt, and we asked them to keep the protesters off our backs. All I could get out of them was that the matter was under active consideration.... Active consideration! Sounds like government-speak for doing nothing."

Reaching for the VHF radio that was mounted overhead, just above and to the left of his shoulder, he changed the frequency from the inter-ship one he'd been using to keep the sealing fleet together, to the Canadian Coast Guard Channel, number 22A. The nearest station was located at St. Anthony, near the northernmost tip of Newfoundland, with call sign VCM. *Jonah's Escape's* call sign was VO1 ORZ.

"St. Anthony Coast Guard, St. Anthony Coast Guard, St. Anthony Coast Guard, Victor, Charlie, Mike, this is Jonah's Escape, Jonah's Escape, Jonah's Escape, Victor Oscar One Oscar Romeo Zulu. Over."

There was a delay of several minutes.

"Why don't they answer?" asked Jones.

"They will," replied the skipper. "This channel is continuously monitored. They'll be looking for an open channel for us to continue on." The radio was silent for a few more minutes, enough to start Jones fidgeting but he had the sense to remain quiet. Finally, there was a response.

"Jonah's Escape, Jonah's Escape, this is St. Anthony Coast Guard, St. Anthony Coast Guard, Victor, Charlie, Mike. Go to channel seven one. I say again, seven one. Over."

"St. Anthony Coast Guard, St. Anthony Coast Guard, this is Jonah's Escape. Roger, switching to seven one."

The skipper switched the radio channel to 71.

"St. Anthony Coast Guard, this is Jonah's Escape. Over."

When the Coast Guard operator responded, the skipper asked to make a radiotelephone call to the St. John's RCMP. When that connection was made, it took him some time to explain who he was and why he was calling, but he was eventually referred to someone that seemed to know about the sealers' request for help.

"The CO approved sending a squad to keep the peace and we have requested the Coast Guard supply the transport. Over."

"Well, we're half a day's sailing from the Front now, and in the morning, I expect to see the *Ocean Saviour* run up on the ice right in front of us. So, where the hell are your people? Over."

"What is your position? Over."

As the skipper provided their position, Jones left the wheelhouse for the open stern of the boat, where he could have a smoke and prepare himself. When he retuned, fifteen minutes later, the skipper was just wrapping up his call.

"Roger. Jonah's Escape, Victor Oscar One Oscar Romeo Zulu. Out," the skipper said, switching the radio back to the general channel for monitoring and alerts, channel 16.

"Any luck?" Jones asked.

"Well, for once, they listened to us. The Mounties have sent a squad. They're on the Coast Guard ship *John A. Macdonald*, and they're only about 30 nautical miles behind us. We'll be at the Front before noon tomorrow."

***

March 15, 1979
The Front, southeast of Labrador

Sure enough, in the morning sunrise, some 60 hours after having left St. John's, we arrived within sight of the ice pack.

From the Monkey Island deck, using binoculars we could just make out some of the seals. As we approached the icepack, several things happened in fairly rapid succession. First, the ship's small helicopter was launched to check the position of the sealing fleet.

Not long after that, we were overflown by a Canadian Coast Guard Grumman S-2 Tracker. This was a rather squat-looking, twin engine aircraft of the kind used by the Royal Canadian Navy for anti-submarine warfare[59].

Someone said, "Well, they certainly know where we are now."

After the plane had passed, Captain Webb came on the ship's intercom to say that the sealing fleet had been spotted about four hours behind us, that the Coast Guard plane meant that the police were probably not far behind the sealers. He added that we would shortly be driving our ship into the icepack, so everyone was to get ready to get out onto the ice.

A few minutes later, Ginger and I were in our cabins gathering our boots and parkas when Captain Webb came back on the intercom saying "Sound the collision alarm."

Moments later, we heard one of the bridge crew say "Brace for collision!" over the intercom. This was immediately followed by the sound of the ship's general alarm: an impossible-to-ignore seven short blasts followed by one long blast.

"I'm glad we got off the Monkey Bridge before that alarm went off, or we'd be hard-of-hearing for a while," I commented to Ginger.

The general alarm sent all crew members to their designated muster stations, while the rest of us braced ourselves as best we could.

The tension mounted as our ship sailed straight at the icepack, but we didn't have long to wait before the ship began to shudder and we could hear a grinding noise. This only lasted for a few minutes, before the ship's motion stopped completely, the engines were shifted down to idle, and everything went silent.

Our ship had been driven partway into the ice.

When we returned to our favourite viewing positions atop the Monkey Bridge, we watched as the crew pushed out a ramp from a lower cargo hatch. With the ramp in place, a small cascade of snowmobiles and trailers were driven down the ramp and onto the ice.

"Looks like no dog-sleds on this trip," I said to Silver, who looked disappointed. I explained to Ginger that several of our northern adventures of the previous few years had involved travelling by dogsled, and that as a former sled-dog himself, he probably missed it.

As we continued to watch, the ship's crew and some of the staff from the Ocean Saviour Foundation busied themselves setting-up tents for the staging of media equipment and installing stoves that would be needed later to warm-up protesters and media alike.

Although we had enjoyed cool springtime temperatures in St. John's, at the Front it was freezing – literally. The overnight low had been -21 °C (-6 °F) and the forecast high for the day was -9 °C (+15 °F). Being on the ocean, it was a humid cold, making it harder to block, and it was windy. And if that wasn't enough, the sky was completely overcast and there was a possibility of snow later in the afternoon.

Having grown up in Ontario, I was well used to cold, high-humidity winters and had brought suitable clothing. Silver, of course, was probably going to enjoy the cold, I thought, having grown-up in Alaska and being genetically well adapted to cold and snow. Vivian, I knew, was used to the warmer climates of the continental United States, but we had recently shared an adventure in the Northwest Territories[60] above the Arctic Circle, in the dead of winter, and I knew she could take care of herself.

Ginger I wasn't so sure about, not so much because of the stereotypes about spoiled movie stars but because I knew she was used to the warmer Pacific Coast climates of southern British Columbia and California. My fears were heightened when she came into my cabin fully decked-out, saying "How do I look?"

She was wearing new and expensive-looking jacket, ski-pants, and boots. "You look great," I said, and then closed in for a closer look. I needn't have worried, however. The jacket and pants were simply stylish (and expensive) models of a top-ranked ski clothing brand, and hidden under the flared cuffs of her ski pants was a pair of top quality felt-pack boots that would keep her feet warm in far colder temperatures than we were about to encounter.

Seeing me relax, she started teasing me immediately.

"Satisfied? Or is your naïve and spoiled movie star completely out of tune with where we are and where we're going?"

"Sorry," I said sheepishly, "I should know you better by now, but when you put on your famous actress persona I still get taken in sometimes."

"That's OK," she laughed. "I'm glad you care, but don't worry about me, I grew up in sight of the Rockies – remember? I was skiing in the mountains by the time I was eight."

"Right. Sorry," I repeated. "But seriously, don't forget who I'm looking for out there. If we find him, I want you to promise me that you'll keep out of the way and let Silver and I deal with him. There may be fighting among the protesters and the sealers too, and I want you to be careful to steer clear of that too... You promise?"

"I promise, I promise, but they'll be dangerous for you too, won't they?"

"Yes, but we're trained for this, and it's our job.... Besides, we're dangerous too."

"Yes," she said, looking at me thoughtfully, "somehow I don't doubt that. And armed too, I'll bet, hmmm?"

"Absolutely," I confirmed, patting my left arm under which I had a snub-nosed Smith & Wesson '.38 Special' revolver in a shoulder holster. I also had a few other things with me that I didn't mention.

"It's time," I said, having checked my watch. "You're due in the larger tent for a quick interview with the documentary producers, then they're taking us out to one of the groups of seals so they can try to get some footage of you with a seal pup."

"Sounds like fun," she said, and we made our way down to the opened hatch and ramp, and from there down onto the icepack itself.

Several tents, and even a flagpole and flag, had already been set up.

After everything it had taken to get ourselves onto the trip and then out to the Labrador icepack, standing there for a moment before going into the larger tent felt like an anticlimax. We were standing on ice and snow, under an overcast sky, in the cold with an icy breeze blowing, and for a moment I felt like we could just as easily have been in any of a million other locations in Canada's winter. *Oh well*, I thought, before following Ginger into the tent for a preliminary interview.

The documentary people just wanted to get some footage of Ginger reiterating her feelings about the seals and the hunt, before going out to mingle with them in person. That didn't take long, and soon we were whisked away by several snowmobile-sled combinations.

Suddenly, there we were, and it seemed like there were seals everywhere. In among the adults, were the seal pups with the beautiful white fur. We waited for a moment, while the documentary people got set up, and then Silver and I stayed back while Ginger was filmed walking up to one of the baby seals. When she did, the cameraman moved in close to catch the baby looking up with its big, trusting, brown eyes. Then, Ginger dropped to her knees and took it up in her arms. The producer was ecstatic when she leaned over and, with tears in her eyes, kissed the baby seal on the nose.

After that the other reporters asked Ginger to give them some poses with the seal pups for their still cameras. It was about -12 °C (+10 °F), so most of the pictures were close-up showing Ginger with her hood up, holding a seal pup in her arms, and her breath freezing into tiny droplets and crystals when she exhaled. There would be no mistaking that she was out in the cold, and not in some artificial movie set.

Most of the protestors next took up cans of red or green spray paint and made sure that the media recorded them saving a hundred seal pups by spraying them, making their pelts commercially valueless.

When the picture-taking was finished, that pretty much concluded phase one of the on-ice events.

As if on cue, we heard a shout and saw much pointing of fingers back towards the ship.

The sealing fleet had arrived.

8 CONFRONTATION

As the sealing fleet prepared to moor its boats, the protesters began to get ready. This mostly involved each being issued a large placard mounted on a stick so they could hold it high and wave it around. They were then organized into a line, roughly two people deep, which stretched across the ice a short distance from one of the larger groupings of seal pups.

I couldn't help noticing the nature of the sticks that were being used to hold up the placards. Every one of them seemed to be made from a hockey stick that had its blade cut off. That meant that not only were the sticks more than strong enough to support the placards, they were strong enough to be used as weapons.

In my university years, I had often played a game called floor hockey. It was played indoors, usually on a basketball court, and in our case the puck was an open, weighted ring. The sticks we used were hockey sticks that had the blade sawed off and the exposed end wrapped with hockey tape. We played with much less padding than is used in ice hockey, usually just hockey gloves and helmets with plexiglass visors. In university, at least, the officiating was generally loose enough that the games could get quite violent and I knew from personal experience what it felt like to be struck with a hockey stick on an unprotected part of the body.

Remembering my floor hockey experiences gave me a bad feeling about a group of nearly 40 protesters and ship's crew that were armed with virtually unbreakable hockey sticks and about to encounter a bunch of angry sealers that would no doubt be armed with their own traditional wooden clubs. Seal-hunting regulations, I knew, specified that a sealer use a hardwood club, 24 to 30 inches in length, because that was considered to be the quickest way to 'humanely' kill a seal.

The media people, for their part, set themselves up in two clusters, one each in front of and to the side of the protesters' line. From these vantage points they would be able to get dramatic shots of the sealers approaching, the protesters blocking, and whatever might come next.

By the time the protesters were set up, the sealers had moored their boats to the edge of the icepack using long lines attached to steel rods or spikes that they hammered into the ice. There were a lot of them, and they divided themselves into three groups. At our particular location on a large sheet of ice, there were three main groups of seals each of which had whelped a large number of pups. Each group of sealers headed for one of these, which meant that two of the groups would be able to immediately begin the killing, while the third would confront the protesters. It might have been my imagination, but it seemed to me that the group making its way toward the line of protesters may have comprised the larger, more heavily built sealers.

Spotting Arne Kristiansen talking to some of the reporters, I went over and asked that he assign someone to take one of the snowmobiles and get Ginger back to the ship where she would be safe. He didn't want to, and it occurred to me that he may have been hoping to place Ginger out in front of the protesters to see what would happen. I was in no mood to waste time arguing with him, and I wasn't ready to break my cover yet so, playing my role as Ginger's assistant I meekly acquiesced and turned away. Then, taking Ginger's arm I guided her over to where Vivian was checking her camera.

"Vivian, I'm going to grab one of those snowmobiles and get Ginger back on the ship. After that, I'll come and join you. OK?"

"Right," she said. "I'll be here."

Steering Ginger towards a cluster of snowmobiles that were standing a little way away, I said "We're heading back to the ship. If I can get one of these things started, get on behind me and we'll drive back."

"But I'd like to stay here and help," she said.

"It's too dangerous. The protesters have come prepared for a fight, and those sealers are going to be angry enough to give them one. I think they'll start out by yelling and swearing at each other, but before long some idiot will lose their temper and throw something, or rush the line, and the fighting will break out. There are nearly forty protesters here and that looks like almost the same number of sealers heading straight for them. If things turn violent, the only way I can protect you from that many people is to get you away from them."

"But the protesters know me now, and the sealers wouldn't hurt me, would they?"

"Not normally, no. But when people lose their temper and fights break out anything can happen. Sometimes people start swinging at anything within reach. The safest place for you right now is on the ship. OK?"

"OK, I guess."

"Besides, it's your inner Liz that wants to stay. No one will expect your Ginger persona to hang around."

Fortunately, the snowmobiles had been left with the keys in their ignitions so all I had to do was start one, check the fuel status, make sure Ginger was holding on to me, and go. Steering the machine in a wide arc, we quickly left the protesters and drove well away from all the groups of people. Only then did I make a turn and steer a broad arc towards the *Ocean Saviour*. I didn't have to worry about Silver, he simply let me break a trail with the snowmobile and ran along behind us on the packed track in the snow.

When we reached the ship, I jogged up the ramp and asked the crewmember that was standing guard to call for Sam. When he arrived at the cargo hatchway, I took another close look at him.

"Sam, you have the look of a navy man about you. Were you in the service?"

He straightened up just that little bit before answering. "Royal Canadian Navy ma'am. Petty officer, first class. Served 25 years before 'retiring' so to speak."

"I thought so. You have the manner of an experienced seaman and the tattoos on your biceps aren't completely faded yet." I took out my wallet and showed him my badge and ID. "I need your help PO. There's a fight brewing out there on the ice and I need to go back there, but we need to keep Miss Brandt here safe, that's why I brought her back to the ship."

"Don't you worry, Corporal, she'll be safe here with me." He looked over at Ginger, who flashed him a look that made him stand up even straighter, if that were possible.

"Please just keep calling me Alex. Besides, I'd like to keep my real identity secret just a little bit longer, OK?"

"Your secret is safe with me ma'am… Alex."

"OK then. Ginger, promise me you'll stay with Sam OK? That way, I'll be able to go do what I have to do without worrying about you the whole time."

"I promise, Alex," she said. "But you have to tell me all about it later."

"Count on it," I said, as I ran back down the ramp.

"Come on Silver, we've got work to do."

"*Grrruph!*" said Silver, standing in readiness while I turned the snowmobile ignition over and pressed the throttle.

When I arrived back where the sealers had been advancing on the protesters, it looked like something out of a Hollywood movie. The two groups were arranged more or less face-to-face, with much yelling, swearing, hand-waving, and brandishing of wooden sticks – hockey stick handles in the case of the protesters, and long clubs in the case of the sealers. The protest placards, I noticed, were rapidly disappearing leaving the hockey sticks looking like what they had become: weapons. Meanwhile, the documentary film crew had their camera set up on a large tripod and were busily filming everything, and the reporters were equally busy taking still photographs and/or brandishing microphones attached to shoulder-slung tape recorders.

Leaving the snowmobile parked some distance from the crowd, I took the precaution of removing and pocketing the key – I thought I might need that snowmobile before long – and set out to search for Vivian.

I found her hovering at the edge of one of the media groups.

"Any sign of Major Jones?" I asked.

"Not yet," she replied.

"How about if we try walking just behind the lines of sealers. If you can hold your camera up and make it look like you're just taking pictures, I'll scan the sealers and we can see if Silver can pick up his scent."

"Ok", she replied, "But here, pin this to your parka. This should keep them from attacking us." She handed me a large laminated white card bearing the word PRESS in large black letters. It had a pin attached to the back, which I used to attach it to the front of my parka.

The scene was rapidly becoming chaotic. While I'd gone to the ship and back, the sealers had advanced on the protesters and, while the media cameras clicked and rolled, the confrontation followed a predictable pattern. First there were exchanges of angry words and calls for the other side to disperse and "go home." This led to even harsher words, and then the pushing and shoving began. From there it was a short step to someone throwing the first punch, and a scattering of fist fights broke out.

Silver, Vivian, and I had been walking several feet behind the rearmost ranks of the sealers during this escalation, but none of us saw or sensed any one matching the description of Major Jones. Vivian and I didn't actually expect to see anything useful, as we assumed that if he were there it would be in disguise. It was Silver's nose that we were counting on.

As several fights broke out, what began as two well-defined lines facing each other disintegrated into a dynamic mass of small clusters. In some clusters, the two sides remained in exchanges of heated words, while in others the physical violence continued. Fortunately, the latter was so far restrained to an ebb and flow of fists and sticks.

It was only as we approached one of the last clusters that Silver tensed, his hackles went up, and he gave a low but menacing growl deep in his throat.

I immediately went down on one knee beside him and tried to make out which man (the sealers all seemed to be male) he was looking at.

"I think it's got to be one of the men right in front of us," I said to Vivian.

"Let's get closer," she replied.

As we moved closer, Silver stayed with me while Vivian moved several steps away and to one side. Silver was continuing to growl, but I couldn't yet make out which man had attracted his attention.

Then one of the men turned to look at us briefly, looked away, then turned his head again and took a closer look. We were just close enough for me to see his expression harden. He immediately pushed himself further into the cluster of sealers and protesters and I lost sight of him.

"He's the one wearing an old army parka!" I called to Vivian, pointing at his last position. "He ducked into the middle of the fray."

Just as I saw her nod, three of the clusters merged into a single mass, and we heard the sharp crack of a small gun. Rather than dispersing the mass of people, this seemed to simply add to the confusion and spur more fighting.

***

Major Jones had joined the sealers in their march toward the protesters, but held himself to the rear so he could watch the engagement and its escalation.

When tensions and anger spilled beyond words and into violence, and as the two lines broke up into clusters, he selected one of the clusters in which the sticks had been turned into weapons and again stayed close, but at the rear – observing the ebb and flow of the emotions and actions that surrounded him.

It was just when he was considering moving in to escalate things further that he happened to look back and spot two people and a dog approaching. Mentally classifying them as reporters, he dismissed them and turned back but... *was there something about that dog?*

He turned back for another, more careful, tactical look. Now he saw what he should have seen the first time. One of the figures was moving sideways, as if to begin a flanking movement. The other stayed with the dog and was clearly in control of it. The dog was looking directly at him and looked angry.

Trouble, he thought. *Time to move.* He immediately turned back and pushed his way into the centre of the cluster of angry people and selected a sealer-and-protester pair that seemed to be acting particularly out of control. He sidled up beside them. From a pocket, he withdrew a Deer Gun. Holding the gun close to his body, and at hip level where it was unlikely to be seen, he aimed a shot right between the two struggling people.

There was a sharp crack, and someone on the other side fell, screaming that they'd been shot. It might have been a sealer or it might, equally, have been a protester. He didn't care, but he did add his voice to the confusion.

"One of them has a gun!" he yelled. "Get them before they can shoot again!"

In another situation, the gunshot and accompanying yells might have caused people to step back in shock and assess what was going on, but in this case, Jones had judged his moment well. What actually happened was that the fighting intensified and bodies jammed in even more closely than they had before. Any semblance of a line had long since been lost. It was now just a mass of sealer-and-protester pairs faced off against each other, rather like happens when a brawl breaks out in a hockey game, except that in this case the use of fists was increasingly giving way to the use of the stout sticks everyone was carrying.

Somewhere in the mass, the person that had been shot must have been lying, bleeding on the ice. Even that was difficult to judge, however, as the stick-swinging had already begun to produce its own casualties, leading to other shapes that were down, huddled on the ice.

Jones, for his part, was slipping through the crowd, his eyes everywhere as he tried to judge whether to risk reloading and taking another shot. He was feeling tempted to do just that, when he heard the roar of medium-sized helicopter approaching. His trained ear told him that the sound wasn't right for the protesters' small spotting helicopter, this was something a bit larger. Then he saw it: a bright red helicopter bearing a diagonal white stripe.

The Coast Guard had arrived, he realized.

Time to leave, thought Jones, correctly guessing that the helicopter was ferrying police officers to the scene of the fighting. With that, he immediately shed his faded army-surplus parka and dropped it onto the ice where it disappeared underneath the jostling fighters. Underneath the parka, he'd been wearing a trendy, bright-red down jacket of the sort that a university-age protester might wear. From one pocket of his insulated pants he brought out a blond wig. Ducking low for a moment, he removed the dark, oil-stained baseball cap he had been wearing and replaced it with the wig. From the other pants pocket he took out the Deer Gun and simply allowed it to fall from his gloved hand as he resumed slithering through the crowd, looking for a way out. He wasn't worried about the loss of the gun; he had brought a second one.

Jones had not forgotten about the suspicious people with the dog. When he exited the large cluster of fighters, he was purposely on the opposite side from them. He began walking away from the crowd and towards the protesters' snowmobiles. As he did so, he heard the blasts of two ships' horns. Looking over towards the *Ocean Saviour*, he saw two Coast Guard ice breakers approaching. That explained the helicopter.

Well back from the crowd now, he was able to observe the side door of the landed helicopter slide open. Out scrambled four Mounties, after which the helicopter immediately took off and headed back towards one of the icebreakers.

Going back for more, thought Jones. *Definitely time to be gone.*

Forcing himself to maintain a walking pace, he continued towards the parked snowmobiles, started one and drove off.

Although disguised like a protester now, he was not headed for the *Ocean Saviour.*

***

Since the gunshot somehow had the effect of compressing the fighters, rather than dispersing them, I could see that there was no way Silver and I were going to be able to get inside the crowd and accomplish anything useful. Motioning to Vivian, I tried to indicate that we were going to try working our way around the outside.

She nodded, and motioned that she was going to work her way around the other side.

As we each skirted the crowd from our own side, I first heard and then saw a Coast Guard helicopter approach and land somewhere near one of the other crowds of fighting people. *Reinforcements*, I thought, wondering whether they would spook our quarry.

Eventually, Silver and I made our way to the far side of the cluster from where we had started, where we met up with Vivian.

"Anything?" she asked.

"No, nothing at all. Let's try going around the side you came from." We did this, and completed the rest of the circle without Silver sensing anything.

"Damn. We've lost him. He's either in the middle somewhere where Silver can't sense him or he's not in this group anymore."

It was only when the noise from the helicopter, returning to one of the icebreakers, faded that Vivian turned her head, saying "Hear that?"

"Hear what?" I asked.

"Sounds like a snowmobile," she said, walking further away from the crowd. After a few moments, she beckoned me with a wave and pointed back toward the ships. "See it?"

Squinting, I could make out two specks in the distance. "A snowmobile and trailer," I said.

"Right. One of the protesters' machines, but it's not heading for the *Ocean Saviour*."

"No, it's not," I agreed. "Where's it going then?"

"What do you want to bet it's Major Jones, heading for the spot where the sealers tied-up their fishing boats?"

"I know better than to bet against you. We'll never catch him before he grabs a boat and casts off, let's go see if the Coast Guard will help us."

As we walked over to where I had parked 'our' snowmobile, we could hear, and then see, the Coast Guard returning to drop off four more police officers. That made eight on the ice so far, which was enough for them to begin dispersing the first cluster of fighters while the helicopter returned to the ship for more.

When we got to our snowmobile, we took off for the icebreakers as fast as we could. As we approached, we could see that one icebreaker had drawn itself up into the ice and right alongside the *Ocean Saviour*, while the other icebreaker had stationed itself broadside against the latter's stern.

The *Ocean Saviour*, at least, wasn't going anywhere for a while.

I steered for the icebreaker that had rammed its way into the icepack.

Laurie Schramm

9 THE CHASE

"Once is happenstance. Twice is coincidence.
The third time it's enemy action."
Auric Goldfinger in:
I. Fleming, *Goldfinger*, 1959

As we approached the icebreaker that had run itself into the ice alongside the *Ocean Saviour*, we could make out the name inscribed on the bow, *John A. Macdonald*[61]. Seen up close, it was huge; twice as long and twice as wide as the *Ocean Saviour*. A ramp had been set up by an open cargo door amidships, so that's where we headed.

Leaving the snowmobile parked to one side, we walked up to the ramp and identified ourselves to the sailor and the officer on duty. They seemed surprised, but didn't question the credentials we showed them, and telephoned our request to see the Captain. It was granted, and the sailor escorted us into the ship and up to the bridge.

When we arrived, a surprisingly young-looking, sandy-haired, blue-eyed man of medium height and build came over to greet us. He was wearing a Lieutenant Commander's epaulettes, and the sailor introduced him to us as Captain Stanford.

Being in plain clothes, I didn't salute him but I introduced Vivian and we both showed him our badges and identification cards.

"So. What brings an undercover Mountie and FBI agent to the coast of Labrador? Something to do with all the fighting that's been going on ashore?"

"Not quite, Sir," I responded. "We came aboard the *Ocean Saviour* looking for a wanted murderer. He wasn't among the ship's crew or passengers, but we did spot him among the sealers so he must have come on one of the fishing boats. Just after we spotted him, there was a shot and he disappeared in the confusion. By the time we spotted him again, he had taken a snowmobile and was headed for the fishing boats. He had too much of a lead on us for us to catch him, so we came here instead. We're hoping you can help us."

"I see," said the Captain, scratching his head. "Well, as you've probably noticed, we're a bit busy right now. We're still ferrying the last of your colleagues over to the scene of the fighting. We brought 15 of them along and the last are going out right now." He pointed to the helicopter, which had just taken off from the flight deck and was heading towards the mass of struggling figures on the ice. "Once they get everyone settled down out there, they'll be making arrests and seizing the protesters' ship[62]. Our mission is to support your colleagues and then tow the ship back to St. John's," he concluded. "That means we need both of our ships right here, for the time being."

"How about your helicopter then? Can you have it take us out so we can at least find the fishing boat and figure out where it's headed?"

While he considered for a moment, Vivian interjected. "Captain, these people out here have broken a few rules, and there's probably going to be some assault charges for people on both sides of the conflict out there on the ice, but this fellow we're after is a murderer. He's already shot people in four countries and killed at least one, maybe more. Now, we think he's shot someone out there on the ice today already. We need to stop him before he strikes again."

"I hear you, Agent Rule, and I'm not against helping you." He sighed, and came to a decision. "Tell you what. We'll have to call this in and get authorization."

"Would it help if my boss in Ottawa called your boss and made an official, high-level request?"

"It might."

"Can I make a radiotelephone call?"

The Captain nodded, took a step back and motioned to one of the bridge crew. "Give him the number you want, and he'll put you through."

The number I gave him was constantly monitored, 24 hours per day, and I gave the duty officer my rank, name, regimental number, and asked for my boss, Staff Sergeant Bob Simpson. "Top priority. I'll hold."

It seemed to take forever, but was probably only five minutes before the duty officer came back on to say, "connecting you now."

When Bob came on the line, I quickly summarized what had happened, where we were, and what we needed. He seemed completely unsurprised and simply asked me to pass the handset to the Captain. The Captain took the handset and moved a few feet away from us. Taking this as a sign that he didn't want to be overheard, we stepped away ourselves and spent a few moments looking out at the trapped *Ocean Saviour* and the mass of figures on the ice, the latter of which seemed to have stopped fighting.

When the Captain hung up the handset, he came over to us. "You forgot to mention that you're with the Security Service."

"I didn't think it was important. Would it have made a difference?" I asked.

"Probably not." He smiled. "Your boss is going to have his Assistant Commissioner call my Assistant Commissioner in St. John's and make a formal request. I'm pretty sure it will be granted." He looked out one of the bridge windows. "Our helicopter is on its way back now. While it's refueling, I'll have you escorted down to the pilots' ready room where you can tell them what you want. Assuming I get a call granting the authorization, I'll have the pilots do whatever you want short of endangering the helicopter or its crew. OK?"

"Thank you, Captain. Much appreciated."

He motioned for one of the bridge crew to escort us, then put out his hand to shake, saying "Good luck."

Just before leaving, I turned back. "Captain, could I make one more request, please?"

He raised an inquisitive eyebrow, then nodded.

"Could we possibly make a quick stop on the *Ocean Saviour*. There's something there I need to bring with us."

He thought for a moment. "The ship hasn't been impounded yet, and it's a police matter in any case, so it's fine with me." He nodded to the bridge officer, saying "See to it."

We were led down two decks to where a ramp had been extended and lowered to the deck of the *Ocean Saviour*. The bridge officer said he'd wait at the ramp for our return and left us to cross on our own.

When we did, I asked the first crewmember we encountered where we could find Sam Hynes. "Officers' and Scientists' Lounge," we were told. As we made our way there, Vivian asked what on earth I'd come back for. "You'll see," I said, mysteriously.

When we reached the lounge, Sam wasn't actually there, but I'd found what I was looking for.

"Alex!" said Ginger. "What's going on? Everyone is so tense and nervous!"

"There's been fighting. Our quarry was there and shot someone, but he got away. By the time we spotted him again, he was about to grab a fishing boat and get away. We couldn't get to him in time, so we came here, and we're going to go after him in a Coast Guard helicopter. Do you want to come with us?"

"What? ... Yes, of course."

I put a hand up. "Not so fast. You need to understand your options first. If you stay here it will be safer, but the other police are going to impound the ship and tow it back to port. The Captain and crew are certainly going to be arrested, and maybe some of the protesters, media, and sealers too. It's an offence just to observe the seal hunt this close without a permit, so they might arrest you too. It's possible there could be violence when the arrests begin.

"On the other hand, we're chasing a murderer and I don't know what's going to happen. We might not find him, or we might find him and simply alert other people so they can close in on him. On the other hand, we might end up going after him ourselves. It could be dangerous for you if you come with us."

"So, it could be dangerous either way," she said. I nodded, and watched her face as she thought for a moment, her actress persona momentarily discarded. "I take it you're not really a reporter?" she asked Vivian.

"No. FBI. I couldn't tell you before... sorry."

Ginger just nodded again, then came to a decision. "I want to come with you," she said in a firm voice.

"OK?" I said to Vivian. She knew what I was really asking. Bringing a civilian along could complicate things for us.

"OK with me," she said.

"OK then, put some warm clothes on," I continued. "If you have anything valuable with you here, you can bring it if it will fit in your pockets."

Sam caught up with us when we were at Vivian's stateroom getting her outer clothing and boots, and I briefly explained what we were doing.

He wasn't one for small talk. "Good luck then," he said, "come visit me in jail sometime."

"You're practically a bystander here. At worst, the judge will give you a fine and send you on your way. Thank you, Sam, for looking after us."

Once Ginger had offered her thanks as well, we went back to the coast guard ship.

As we went up the ramp to the *John A Macdonald*, the bridge officer looked surprised to see Ginger with us but didn't say anything. "She's coming with us," I said. "Could you take us to the pilots' ready room please?"

"Yes Ma'am," was all he said, and he led us there.

Along the way, Vivian sidled up to me and said, in a low voice, "You trying to keep her safe, or keep her from being arrested?"

"Both," I whispered back. "She stuck her neck out to help us and I don't want anything to happen to her. You OK with that?"

"Oh, sure. Just curious."

When we reached the ready room, the helicopter had obviously returned, as the pilots were there waiting for us.

After introductions had been made, we briefly explained what we were doing. "If the Captain gets the authorization he needs, then we'd like your help finding the fishing boat without him spotting us, figuring out where he's heading, and then get there before he does, also without being spotted. Can you do that?"

They both nodded, then one of the pilots explained that the

helicopter had a bench seat with places for three people, in the cabin behind the pilot and copilot seats.

"What about Silver?" I asked, nodding to where he was sitting patiently.

"No problem. He can lie on the deck at your feet."

Meanwhile, the other pilot had pulled out a chart of the area, and spread it out on a table. "OK," he said, "we are here, about 50 nautical miles east Labrador's southeastern coast. That's about 57 road miles."

"You already know how long it takes to sail here from St. John's," said the other pilot. "If your guy is in a hurry, he'll head for something a lot closer. The nearest options for him are to head WNW to Mary's Harbour in Labrador, though he'll have to go around the ice." He pointed to its location. "That's about 65 nautical miles away. If he can make 13 knots, he'll be there in 5 hours."

"Is there much there?" I asked.

"It's a town of several hundred people. They have an airport and there's a highway. If he can steal or rent a plane he can fly almost anywhere. If he gets a vehicle, it would be a 25-hour drive to Sept-Iles, Quebec, or else he could drive south and take the ferry to Brig Bay, then continue down either coast, but it's a long way to St. John's – 12 to 13 hours at least."

"OK. What else?"

"Well, he could be heading WSW to St. Anthony in Newfoundland. That's over here on the map, about 60 nautical miles away. If he goes there, he'll be just under 5 hours. St. Anthony is a larger town of more than a thousand people. It's a main service and supply centre for northern Newfoundland and southern Labrador, and it has an airport too.

"Or, he could go SW to Cook's Harbour. That's here. It's actually a bit closer, less than 60 nautical miles away. If he goes there, he'll be about four and a half hours, but it's much smaller, maybe a hundred people or so and no airport."

"So, it sounds like the most likely spots are St. Anthony or Mary's Harbour," I suggested.

"Can he fly an aircraft?" asked one of the pilots. I looked to Vivian.

"We know he can fly a helicopter, even a big one. I don't know whether he can fly a fixed-wing or not, but I wouldn't bet against it."

"He really could take the boat anywhere down the coast," said one of the pilots. They wouldn't have come all the way from St. John's without enough fuel to get back."

"That's right, but we have to start somewhere," said Vivian.

"Can you take us up and look for the boat?" I asked.

"If the Captain says so, we can. I'll check," said one of the pilots, and then to the other pilot added, "While I'm doing that, why don't you take them to see what's on the radar."

"Radar?"

"Sure. If your guy has taken a boat, the radar will have at least shown us his initial heading. That should help. Come on."

Back up on the bridge, the pilot led us to one of the radar screens and asked the operator if she'd seen one of the fishing boats leave.

"I did," she replied. "There's been no other traffic besides the helicopter and one of the boats. I reported it to the Captain, but I'd understood that we weren't worried about the fishing boats. I mostly watched its trace because there's so little else to watch right now."

"What direction was it headed?" asked the pilot.

"South, but then it pretty much has to either go north or south to get around the icepack. Look here, I'll show you." She pointed to a dot on the screen. "That's your boat right there, about six nautical miles south of our position."

Thanking her, we left the bridge and headed for the helideck where we were met by the other pilot.

"You ladies seem to have some pull in high places," he announced. "We're to give you all possible assistance short of endangering the helicopter or the people in it."

"Great," I said. "Let's go find him."

"We're not fully fueled up yet, so why don't you go grab a cup of coffee and we'll let you know when we can take off."

A crewmember was assigned to show us to the main galley, where the three of us were able to get coffee, and a bowl of water for Silver. Twenty minutes later one of the pilots came to get us. They were ready to go.

When we reached the helicopter, he said, "Let's get you settled in. I brought you the chart we were looking at. We have our own in the cockpit. Once we've found him, this will make it easier for us to discuss what to do after that."

With that, we were guided to the helicopter, which they called a Bo 105[63]. Once we were all buckled in (except for Silver, of course) we were given headsets with boom microphones, and soon we had lifted off and left the three ships far behind.

Although Major Jones had about an hour and a half's head start on us, the pilots had estimated the fishing boat's speed at about 13 knots, whereas the helicopter's cruising speed was 110 knots. As a result, it only took about 25 minutes for the pilots to find the fishing boat.

"There he is," the co-pilot's voice crackled over the intercom. He was looking through binoculars. "Right where he's supposed to be."

"We'll keep well back so he doesn't hear us. I'm going to veer off and circle for a little while. Any minute now, he'll be turning west if he's heading for any of the nearby ports. If not, he'll keep heading more or less south."

It was hard to be patient while the helicopter turned back and flew in a broad circle. Vivian and I, at the windows, kept looking out as if trying to spot the boat. We both knew that we were flying the wrong way, and in any case the pilots were keeping us well back, but there was really nothing else for us to do.

Finally, we had closed the circle and the co-pilot was scanning the horizon with his binoculars again.

"There," he said, pointing to our right. "He's heading due west. He could be trying to make for St. Anthony. That'll be about 50 nautical miles."

So, nearly four hours, I estimated. "Are you OK with us hanging around in the background until we're sure of his destination?"

"As long as we have fuel, we can," answered the pilot. "Fuel status gives us another three hours. After that, we'll have to land at St. Anthony for fuel, whether your target is going there or not."

"OK, thanks. Can we make a radiotelephone call from here?"

"Sure. Who do you want to call?"

"The RCMP detachment at St. Anthony."

"All right, Stand by."

Looking across at Vivian, I said, "This will make their day."

When the connection was made, I identified myself, gave a brief summary of what was going on, and concluded with a request for assistance. Fortunately, the NCO[64] in Charge of the detachment was there, so I was able to get a rapid confirmation that there would be backup waiting for us at the airport in two hours, and that they would wait for us for at least another hour after that.

The pilots, who had been listening in on the call agreed to keep circling behind the fishing boat – close enough to observe its course but far enough away to be out of hearing. Since every fishing boat would be equipped with binoculars, we would have to take a chance on Jones not being able to scan the skies well enough to spot us. The odds were in our favour, since the circling would ensure that there would only be brief intervals in which we would be distinguishable through binoculars.

For the next two and a half hours Ginger and Silver were very patient, with Ginger seeming to enjoy the views. Vivian and I, for our parts, were getting pretty uncomfortable between the waiting, the noise and vibrations, and the poorly padded bench seating. On the other hand, every close of a circle confirmed that Jones was heading for either Cook's Harbour or St. Anthony. Even if Jones somehow guessed that he was being followed, Vivian and I both felt that would make for an airport where he could hire or steal something to fly him out of the area.

"He's changed heading since our last sweep," reported the co-pilot, "he's now heading north. That means he's probably intending to bypass Cook's Harbour. The next nearest harbour is St.

Anthony. That's less than 20 nautical miles from his current position. All he has to do is cross the head and then turn southwest."

"OK, can you head for St. Anthony without him seeing us?"

"Can do. We can head due west, cross overland, then turn north and be there in 30 minutes."

"Great. Let's do it, please."

The pilot's response was a sharp banking turn to the left and an acceleration back up to cruising speed. Ten minutes later, we could see the Newfoundland coast. We actually flew right past Cook's Harbour, and then the pilot turned more or less north and we got a good view of Newfoundland's most northern terrain as we headed straight for St. Anthony.

When we landed, three police vehicles pulled up to the helicopter: two highway patrol cars and a Chevy Suburban SUV. When we climbed out of the helicopter, we had just a moment to stretch before the NCO from the detachment, a Sergeant, came forward to meet us.

"Alex Houston," I said, reaching out my hand to shake.

"Al Donaldson," he responded, with a firm handshake. "Welcome to St. Anthony."

I introduced Vivian, Ginger, and Silver.

He was polite to each, but his voice increased in warmth when he recognized Ginger.

"How did you get involved in all of this Miss Brandt?" he asked.

"I'll tell you everything later, but basically it was me that snuck Alex aboard the *Ocean Saviour* as my assistant. Silver too, of course. Alex's boss in Ottawa is my uncle. It was all his idea."

"Staff Sergeant Bob Simpson," I supplied.

"This is starting to sound like a scene out of a movie script," said Al, but he smiled to show he was amused, not irritated. "By the way," he said, turning back to me, "I've heard about you."

"You have?" I asked, surprised.

"We have a friend in common, Mike Morrison – we trained together and still keep in touch. It's a small world in The Force, right? Anyway, he's told me a lot about you.... He's a Sergeant now."

"That's great news, I'll send him a note. He was my supervisor on my very first posting[14]. I learned a lot from him, and we became friends too."

Al smiled. "We'll have to compare notes later too. How much time do we have before your suspect arrives?"

I looked at my watch. "According to the pilots, almost exactly one hour."

"So, how do you want to do it?"

I took a deep breath. "I'll tell you what I was thinking, but you know the local layout, so please pitch in here.... If he doesn't think we're on to him, then I imagine he'll just pull up at one of your main docks and then look for a vehicle or aircraft. If he suspects we're following him then he'll try something tricky. He's a former CIA-officer turned mercenary *provocateur*, and he's good at disguises. How much help can we have?"

"This is a small detachment, just me and four constables. One is off sick and one is on a case out of town. That leaves three of us. We could place one man in a car at the lighthouse that overlooks the entrance to the harbour. He can then describe by radio every boat that comes into the harbour. If your timing is right, there won't be many boats coming in at that time of day. Then, you and Constable Ross here could cover the Municipal Dock, which is the most likely, and Agent Rule and I could cover the Ministry of Transport (MOT) Dock, which is the next most likely."

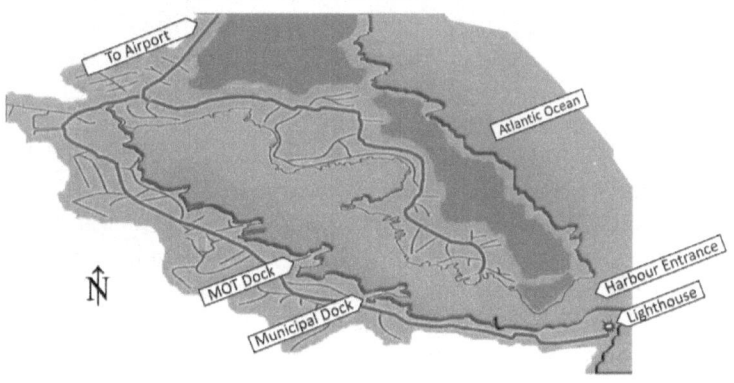

St. Anthony Harbour

Vivian and I agreed to this, so we all went for a quick cup of coffee, over which we described the boat as best we could. "It's a fishing boat. All we could see from a distance, was that it has a white cabin with a blue hull, it's probably 50 to 60 feet in length, and it has one trolling boom on each side.... I know that's not a very unique description."

Donaldson nodded. "It'll be enough."

We didn't linger over coffee, as we wanted to be in position well before our estimate of the time Major Jones might reach the harbour.

The Municipal Dock was the first major docking area for boats entering the harbour. When Constable Ross, Silver and I reached it, we agreed that Silver and I would wait in the car until we received a radio message that a boat matching our description was entering the harbour. Then, Silver and I would stroll out on the dock and pretend we were just out for a casual walk. Constable Ross, who was in uniform, would stay out of sight and watch for my signal. If I put my arm up and straightened my hair twice in a row, that would be the signal that Jones was indeed on the boat. He would then call all the rest in to back us up.

It was a long 45 minutes before the radio crackled and the constable at the lighthouse reported a boat matching our description approaching the mouth of the harbour. After another 15 minutes, the constable radioed again to say that the white and blue boat had entered the harbour and was motoring close to its southern side, towards the Municipal Dock. Sergeant Donaldson acknowledged the message, and instructed the constable to stay where he was and watch for other boats.

It was breezy and cold, as Silver and I began our walk along the dock. When we reached its end, we stopped for a while and watched until we could see the white and blue boat coming our way. Then, we walked back to the shore. I was planning to stroll the dock once more, but only when the boat was lining itself up alongside. Then Silver and I would just 'happen' to be strolling along when Major Jones hopped out to tie it up.

Things went approximately according to plan, at first. The boat slowed as it approached, then turned to come alongside the dock and manoeuvered back and forth a bit to get into position. Silver and I had strolled quite close to the boat when a figure hopped off with a mooring line in hand and went to tie it to a bollard on the dock. It was a male, but something wasn't right. I could only see him from the back, but he seemed too thin to be Major Jones, and his movements seemed more like those of a very young man, or teenager, than those of a fiftyish-year-old man. Whomever he was, Silver wasn't reacting to him at all. Making a conscious effort not to raise either arm, I decided to wait and watch.

When he had secured the bow line, the man jumped back up onto the boat and then hopped off again, this time with a stern line in hand, and he went and secured it to another bollard. Silver and I strolled closer, but I kept my distance from the boat itself and made sure I remained in clear view of Constable Ross. If this was some stranger, then it seemed probable that the Major was still on board the boat.

When the figure finished securing the stern line, rose and turned, it was a teenager I'd never seen before.

I was close enough to speak without raising my voice. "Good afternoon," I said, with a smile. "Was it rough out on the water today?"

"Not really, but it was still a bit of an adventure."

"Oh really, why?"

"I'm really sorry, ma'am. I know it's not polite, but I can't stay and talk to you – I need to go ashore and call the police."

"Really!" I said, "what's wrong?"

"You won't believe it, but I was hijacked. A man with a gun, hijacked the boat and made me bring him here."

"My goodness, what a strange thing to do. Is he on the boat then? Are we in danger right now?"

"Oh no," he replied. "The man left just as we were entering the harbour. That's why I have to go call the police right now."

As he moved to go past me, I said. "Hang on just a moment, please, the police are already here. I dug into one pocket and took out my badge and ID to show him. "Corporal Houston, RCMP," I said. "You were out at the Front, right?"

That stopped him, and his jaw dropped for a moment.

"Right" he said, when he'd recovered himself. "I was left behind to mind the boat and do some small repairs. Then, out of nowhere, this man came on board and threatened me with a gun!"

"Can you describe the man?"

"Well, he's about my height, say five foot nine, not as skinny as I am but not a heavy build either. He has blond hair and blue eyes. When he came on board the boat he had long, blond hair and he was wearing a fancy bright red jacket, but the long hair was a wig. He tossed it overboard and his hair is still blond but cut short. He left the red jacket on the boat and took one of ours – kind of a dark brown work coat."

"That's a good description. Thank you. What did he say?"

"Only that he wouldn't hurt me if I did what he told me. He wanted me to bring him to the closest decent-sized town with a real airport. Then, he said, he'd leave the boat and I could go wherever I wanted after that. I knew that St. Anthony was the business centre for this area, and I figured it would have the largest airport, so I came here."

"And he didn't hurt you?"

"No, but he broke our radio. Wanted to make sure I couldn't call for help later, I guess."

"OK. Now, how and where did he leave the boat?"

"He made me slow down and stop just after we entered the harbour. Then I had to help him lower our dingy over the side and he took off in it. After he left, I came straight here, to the closest pier I could find, so I could call the police."

"And there's no one else on the boat?"

"No ma'am."

"Ok then, would you please come with me so we can call this in. The others may have more questions for you."

He agreed and the three of us walked back to the police SUV where Constable Ross was waiting. As we walked, I asked him for his name, it was James MacDonald.

When we all got in the SUV, I got on the radio and explained what had happened and what I'd learned, so that everyone involved could hear the same story at once.

"What does the dingy look like?" asked Sergeant Donaldson.

"It's a 15-foot Zodiac, red, with a black, 30 hp Mercury motor," said James.

"Standby," said Sergeant Donaldson. "I brought binoculars with me." There was a pause as he scanned the harbour, which fortunately was quite narrow so it was easy for him to see the northern shore from his position.

"Got it!" he said, with satisfaction. "Red Zodiac with black Mercury motor. It's heading west along the northern shore."

"I bet he'll put in somewhere, grab a vehicle and make for the airport," I said. "James said he specifically wanted to be landed somewhere with a reasonable sized airport."

"Agreed," said Sergeant Donaldson. Addressing the constable at the lighthouse, he instructed him to drive to the junction of East Street (leading out of the town's business district) with North Street (the road Jones would have to take to get to Highway 430 and the airport, which led northward out of town, before turning westward to the airport). "When you get there, park somewhere out of sight and stay on the radio."

"We're going to take a quick look on board then we'll join you," I added.

"No offense," I said to James, "but I have to be absolutely sure that this guy didn't force you to tell us a fairy-tale while he stayed in hiding on the boat. Would you be willing to come back with me and show me around?"

"Sure," he said. "No problem."

"I'll join you," said Constable Ross. I knew that he meant that he was coming along 'just in case,' and I nodded in appreciation.

As it turned out, my extra caution was unnecessary.

When we reached the boat, I looked Silver directly in the eyes and asked him to search for the 'evil man' just like I had when we were out on the icepack. I know it sounds a bit silly, but he knew what I wanted.

With Silver in the lead, James and I followed. Constable Ross followed too, but kept himself several yards behind us at all times.

Silver sniffed around everywhere, pausing only for James to reach out and open bulkhead doors for him. The only thing he found was the red jacket, which had been stuffed down, out of sight, between a mattress and the ship's hull.

I apologized again to James if I'd seemed to doubt his story, and asked whether we could take the red jacket with us. He agreed, and Constable Ross asked him to wait for us at a nearby restaurant until someone could return later, to take an official statement from him.

"Do you have any money?" I asked.

"No!" he said, surprised. "I forgot to tell you. He made me give him all the money I had."

"OK. Here's enough so you can have dinner while you're waiting. OK?" I asked, taking some bills out of my wallet.

"Yes. Thank you," he said, seeming surprised that we would help him out that way.

"All part of the service," I quipped, as we thanked him for his help and got back into the police SUV.

A quick radio check brought the news that, while we'd been searching the boat, the Zodiac had been run ashore almost directly across the harbour from Sergeant Donaldson's position. A man matching Jones' description had disembarked and was walking westbound along East Street.

"I think he's hitch-hiking," said the sergeant.

The radio was silent for the few minutes it took us to drive up to where Sergeant Donaldson and Vivian had parked the highway patrol car. We had no sooner pulled up behind them when the radio crackled again. It was Sergeant Donaldson. "Someone's stopped. A late model pickup truck. White, two-door. Looks like nets or something similar sticking up out of the box.... It's moving again and the man... is not in sight. I think the truck picked him up."

The sergeant then instructed the constable at the road junction to watch for the white pickup truck and report which way it was heading. "We're coming to your position now," he concluded.

We were almost in sight of the parked highway patrol car, when the constable on surveillance came on the radio. "White pickup truck matching your description just turned right onto North Street. Two people in the truck. They may be heading for the highway."

"Roger. Follow them but remain out of sight. We're right behind you." Then, to me, he said "What do you think? If we try to stop them now, he'll have a hostage and he may force a chase on the highway rather than stopping. If we let him get to the airport, we may be able to catch him out in the open."

"I'd say try to get him out in the open. Vivian, if he thinks he's surrounded with no chance of escape, can we get him to surrender?"

"As long as we give him time to think it through, yes. He may even think that he has enough leverage or 'friends in high places' to get off scot-free," she replied.

"I think we should warn the pilots of the Coast Guard helicopter though," I suggested.

"Do you know their callsign?"

I provided it, and Sergeant Donaldson asked his dispatcher to contact the helicopter and warn them that the man we were chasing might try to hijack their machine.

The drive to the airport took a little over half an hour. About halfway there, Sergeant Donaldson slowed his car so we could pass in the SUV, explaining, "We're well back, but if he's been watching he'll now see a truck behind him now instead of a car."

As we turned off the highway, I could see that there was a main terminal building, with several hangars spaced out on each side of it. The pickup truck had turned towards a cluster of three buildings to the right of the terminal. As soon as it was out of sight, Sergeant Donaldson radioed his two constables to say that he would join Vivian and I behind the centre building, and that they should go and park behind each of the other two. If the white truck passed either of them, they were to stop it, make sure there was only one person in it, make sure they were OK, get their name and the truck's licence plate number and let it go. Otherwise, they were to stay close to their vehicles and their radios.

For our part, we agreed that Vivian, Silver, and I would go after Jones, while the sergeant would stay back out of sight, and that Ginger was to stay in the police SUV and not get out under any circumstances. Ginger didn't like it, but she agreed.

Jogging to the front of the centre hangar, Vivian and I stopped for a look around. Sure enough, the white pickup truck was stopped not far ahead of us on the tarmac and just beside it was a small, fixed-wing airplane. Major Jones was standing by the airplane, and appeared to be pointing a gun at another person who was climbing down, out of the plane. As we watched, the person from the plane was waved over to the truck, got in, and the truck drove off. Jones then walked around the front of the plane and bent down to remove the wheel chock from the wheel that was furthest away from us.

"Let's go," said Vivian, "we'll never get a better chance than this."

"Right," I agreed, and turned to motion to Sergeant Donaldson that we were going to approach Jones.

As we walked toward the airplane, Vivian and I moved apart by about ten feet, and I told and motioned Silver to sweep out to one side so he could approach from one flank. We had done this manoeuver so many times before that he immediately knew what to do.

As he rose from his crouch, holding a wheel chock in one hand,

Major Jones immediately saw us. Tossing the chock to one side, he quickly went to pull the chock from the second wheel, which he also tossed to one side.

By this time, Vivian and I were close enough to call out to him without having to yell.

"Major Jones!" I called out.

He stopped and looked at me, his hand reaching into a pocket, from which he withdrew a pistol.

"Corporal Houston, RCMP," I explained, "and this is Special Agent Rule, FBI."

"What do you want?" he asked calmly.

"I'm afraid this is the end of the line for you. I need you to drop your gun and surrender," I responded, drawing my own gun at the same time.

"I saw you, just for a moment, out on the icepack. How'd you get ahead of me?"

"Coast Guard helicopter from the icebreaker. It's over on the other side of the airport but it hasn't refueled yet, just so you know."

"He nodded. I thought it might not have been refueled, that's why I came for this plane instead.... How'd you know I'd be at the Front in the first place?"

"We didn't. We just started staking out organized protests, playing the odds that you'd eventually show up at one."

"You've been at this for a while then."

I knew he was buying time to think, but that was alright. I wanted him to be calm and rational. "Yes. Quite a while, and between us, Agent Rule and I followed a lot of blind alleys before spotting you this morning."

"And you think I'm just going to surrender to you now? To just one Mountie?"

"And one FBI agent," said Vivian, brandishing a pistol of her own.

"And there are uniformed officers out of sight... You're surrounded, you see."

"Maybe," he said, "maybe not. I only see the two of you."

"OK. Even if you don't believe me about the backup, Agent Rule and I are both armed, as you see, and we're both pretty good shots at this range. I know you have the training and experience to make good tactical decisions. How do you see this one? We're well enough separated to keep you from jumping both of us, we can each fire multiple rounds without stopping to reload, and... I see that you have another of your Deer Guns there."

He flinched, startled that I'd seen that.

"According to my friend here, that's a single shot weapon. If you shoot one of us, the other won't give you time to reload."

"Maybe I'll take my chances," he said, pointing his gun straight at me. Vivian and I had continued to walk towards him while this discussion was taking place, and we were now close enough that none of us was likely to miss if any shooting started.

I was debating what to say next, when Jones' attention shifted to something behind Vivian and I. As I turned my head slightly to see what he was looking at, I expected that it would be Sergeant Donaldson. He had, in fact, made an appearance in the front of the hanger, but that wasn't the focus of Jones' attention – it was Ginger.

"Ginger Brandt?" he said. "What's she doing here?"

I didn't answer him. Instead, I gave a specific hand signal to Silver, who had crept up close to Jones from one side, and just out of his line of sight.

Without making a sound, Silver sprang into action. He took three large bounds and jumped at Jones, closing his mouth on Jones' gun hand and letting his weight drag Jones down on one knee.

I had started running forward as soon as Silver had clamped his jaws on Jones, so that I was able to quickly close the distance between us.

"Drop the gun Major. He's strong enough to tear your hand apart if you don't, and if you try to hurt him..." Jones had raised his other arm, his hand balled into a fist. "Then I'll shoot you myself."

He took a close look at me, decided I was serious - which I was - and then exhaled sharply, lowered his raised arm, and dropped the gun.

"Silver. Grab the gun," I ordered. Silver released his grip, took up the Deer Gun in his jaws and came over to stand beside me.

"Good boy, Silver. Well done," I praised, as Vivian walked over to see about bandaging Jones' bleeding hand with a handkerchief.

Sergeant Donaldson and Ginger had both run up to us by this time, as I was saying "Major Jones, I arrest you for assault with a weapon. You need not say anything. You have nothing to hope from any promise or favour, and nothing to fear from any threat, whether or not you say anything. Anything you do or say may be used as evidence against you at your trial."

"Trial," he snorted. "There'll be no trial. You mentioned military tactics earlier. I may be surrendering now but I have friends in high places. They'll get me off, and they'll get me home."

10 EPILOGUE

Sergeant Donaldson had promptly radioed his other two constables when the action had started, so Jones was quickly searched, handcuffed, and placed in the back of one of the highway patrol cars.

Ginger had rushed up to give me a big hug.

"You promised to stay behind in the SUV," I admonished.

"Yes, but I was worried about you, and then I worried even more when it looked like he was going to shoot you. So, I thought if I could distract him for just a moment, that you'd find a way to get the upper hand on him – and I was right!"

"Yes, and thank you. But you took an awful risk. What you did was brave and foolish. Vivian and I, and the Sergeant and his men, were perfectly capable of handling him."

"Sure, with you maybe getting shot in the deal! I don't care about this Jones guy. I care about you."

"Well, thank you Ginger. As it turned out, you were a big help. He forgot all about Silver for a moment, and didn't see him coming until it was too late."

Sergeant Donaldson had heard some of our conversation, as he walked up to us.

"I agree with what they said about being brave but foolish Miss Brandt, but boy did you distract him! You're not like your TV character at all!"

"Not dumb and helpless, you mean Sergeant? Well, if you want to do me a favour then keep it to yourself, please. I don't want my fans to suspect that I'm anything else and, if you can, please keep my name out of the papers as much as you can, OK? And please, call me Ginger."

"Whatever you say, Miss Ginger. The reporters will probably find out you were here today, and they can sensationalize that all they want I guess, but we'll keep the details of your involvement quiet if that's the way you want it."

Vivian had taken possession of the Deer Gun, and showed it to us before handing it over to the sergeant for evidence.

"It's a nasty-looking thing alright," said the sergeant, looking at the gun, which looked even smaller in his large hand. "How many of these things did he have? Must be quite a few to be able to leave them everywhere as calling cards."

"We'll probably never know for sure," said Vivian, "but he probably got all or most of the 150 of them that went missing in Vietnam, and only seven or eight have turned up at crime scenes so far as I know. Our government will be filing an extradition request so we can get him home after your courts are done with him. We'll see what we can pry out of him."

As the police car with Jones in the back drove off, that was the last I ever saw of him. He was placed in cells in the St. Anthony Detachment pending orders on when and where to transport him for a court appearance.

Vivian and I thanked Sergeant Donaldson and his people for their help, and we took some pictures of the sergeant and the remaining constable posing with Ginger, which she promised to sign and return once they were printed. I'm told that the signed and framed photograph she sent them still hangs in the detachment office.

The two Coast Guard pilots, having seen the excitement and recognized us, came over to check on us (when it was safe) and offered to take us back to St. John's once their refueling was complete. That was good of them, as it probably involved stretching their original orders a bit, and we thanked them warmly and accepted.

It was getting late in the day by the time the helicopter took off, and with our adrenaline coming back down a blanket of weariness settled on us. For my part, however, I slept soundly almost all the way to St. John's, the helicopter's noise and vibrations notwithstanding. I'm pretty sure Silver did too. There was one small event that happened just before I fell asleep. We were well out over the ocean when Vivian suddenly leaned forward from her seat, opened a small window that was inset in the side door, and tossed her gun out.

"What was that?" I asked, rhetorically, because I knew very well what it was.

"Oh, nothing important," she said.

"So, tell me, hypothetically speaking of course. If an FBI agent was coming to Canada to work undercover on a dangerous mission, and she felt that it was prudent to have a gun, for self-defense if nothing else, what would she do?"

"You mean if there hadn't been time to get special permits and she didn't want to risk being caught with a gun when she crossed the border into Canada?"

"Exactly."

"Well, I suppose that our hypothetical agent would just innocently cross the border and then go buy one when she was here."

"Yes, but where the hell did you... I mean, where would she even get a gun without a permit, and so quickly too."

"Ah. Well, that part's easy. Our resourceful agent would probably drive to a small-town gun show, scope it out, maybe stand for a few drinks in the local bar, and find out who at the gun show might quietly sell a gun and a box of rounds, for cash, out of the trunk of their vehicle. That kind of thing happens every day in the States, but it happens here too, just not as blatantly."

"And then when the danger has passed?"

"Oh, well then, when the action's past and it's time for the agent to go home, she probably doesn't want to risk crossing the border with it on her then either. She wouldn't want it to fall in the wrong hands, of course, so she'd probably try to dispose of it somewhere no one would ever find it."

"Like at the bottom of the ocean, for example?"

"That would be a good place, don't you think? Even in the one-in-a-million chance that someone found it, as long as it wasn't right away, it would have rusted into uselessness." She gave me a wide-eyed innocent look.

"Remind me never to play poker with you," I said, and went to sleep.

Meanwhile back at the Front, the officers there had established order at the scene of the fighting, and charged several protesters and several sealers with assault. They were later all convicted and fined accordingly. Captain Webb, his entire crew of 24, and the ship's complement of protesters were all charged with being unlawfully within a half mile of the seal hunt. All of them were eventually convicted and fined as well. The media people on the ship were initially charged, but the Crown Prosecutor later dropped their charges. Ginger was never charged, having been judged to have only been there in her capacity of helping the police.

The next day after the return ride in the helicopter, back in St. John's, we said our goodbyes to Vivian, who flew back to the U.S.

That same day, Staff Sergeant Bob Simpson flew in from Ottawa. It was his practice to meet me for a debriefing after each assignment and, in this case, his niece Ginger's presence gave him an added incentive. He followed the whole story with careful attention and, predictably, had a few words for both of us on the subject of taking reasonable but not excessive risks. He was clearly proud of both of us, though, so we knew we weren't in too much trouble, and I knew that he was partly speaking out of his own guilt for having thought up the idea of Ginger's role in the first place. For Silver, of course, he had unequivocal praise, which Silver lapped up like dog treats.

***

Much later, I heard from Ginger that the IAAP paid all the fines for Captain Webb, his crew, Arne Kristiansen, and the protesters and even for the release of the *Ocean Saviour* from impoundment. Ginger told me that, while she had had enough of such protests, the IAAP people were well satisfied with the media exposure they received from the documentary film and news articles, and that they felt the whole adventure had taken them one step closer to ending the seal hunt, or at least the end of the killing of the seal pups.

Perhaps they were right. Although the Canadian government remained slow to make changes, the protests eventually did sway public opinion in Europe. Several years later, in 1983, the European Union banned the sale of whitecoat pelts, and for the first time in the history of the Canadian seal hunt, the kill fell below 100,000 seals. In 1987, the Canadian Government finally halted the commercial hunt for 'whitecoat' harp seal pups.

***

And Major Jones?

The day after his arrest a black, sleek-looking private helicopter landed at the airport in St. Anthony. A man in a three-piece business suit disembarked and took a taxi to the RCMP Detachment where he identified himself as Major Jones' lawyer. The man met with Jones for an hour and a half, then returned to the helicopter and left. The helicopter was later found to have flown under a fictitious registration. Its flight plans were from and to Dulles Airport, Washington, DC.

The next morning, Jones was found dead in his cell. The pathology report cited death due to saxitoxin, a potent neurotoxin known to be used by the CIA.

It seems that Jones' friends in high places took note of his activities, but not with the results that he'd had in mind.

Laurie Schramm

… Alex and Silver will return,
in *An Intimate Mountie*.

Laurie Schramm

SUMMARY

When RCMP Corporal Alexandra Houston and her partner Silver experience a chance encounter with two suspicious characters on the front lawn of Canada's Parliament Buildings, Alex decides to do a little digging. The results take them from the Pacific coast of British Columbia to the Atlantic coasts of Newfoundland and Labrador, on the trail of a professional agitator whose appearances at organized protest events seem to coincide with a trail of violence, injuries, and death.

Laurie Schramm

ABOUT THE AUTHOR

Laurie Schramm comes from an RCMP family, grew up while living in the RCMP Barracks (Depot Division) in Regina, Saskatchewan, and spent several summers working as a civilian for the RCMP while in high school and university. Early personal influences included not only the real-life RCMP culture but also Hollywood's versions via such classics as Rose Marie, and Susannah of the Mounties. Many of the events described in this novel are based on the author's real life, although not necessarily within an RCMP context.

For more information, see Laurier L. Schramm on **Linked** in

and:

www.laurieschramm.ca

or

www.facebook.com/LaurieSchrammBooks

Laurie Schramm

ENDNOTES

1. The Civilian Irregular Defense Group (CIDG) was a covert CIA program that established and supported paramilitary South Vietnamese units for which training and advice were supplied by U.S. Army Special Forces personnel. The main purpose of the CIDGs (at least initially) was to counter insurgency into South Vietnam by the Viet Cong. Boun Enao was the first of many CIDG villages. See E.C. Piasecki, "Civilian Irregular Defense Group: The First Years: 1961-1967," *Veritas - Journal of Army Special Operations History*, **5** *(4)* 2009, pp. 1-10.

2. The CIA Deer gun was made of cast aluminum and carried no identifying markings. It is five inches long and just over four inches tall. The barrel unscrewed for loading of a single 9mm round. After reattaching the barrel, a striker would be cocked to prepare it for firing. A simple, insertable plastic clip served as a safety. The pistol grip was hollow, and could store three rounds plus a metal rod that was used to clear the barrel of a spent case. They were designed to be delivered by airdrop, and were packaged in polystyrene boxes together with three cartridges and pictorial instructions. Although 1,000 Deer Guns were manufactured (in 1964), only about 150 were sent

to South Vietnam "for field testing." All 1,000 of them were supposed to have been destroyed but some examples have survived. The name 'Deer Gun' is thought to have been a codename.

3. "Yards" was a U.S. Army Special Forces nickname for the Montagnard Tribes that formed the first CIDGs. It was meant affectionately. See the reference in endnote #1.

4. U.S. Military Assistance Command, Vietnam (MACV), which by this time had taken over command of the Special Forces-led paramilitary activities from the CIA.

5. Much of this account is fictional, of course, but in real life the Ohio National Guard later claimed that a sniper had fired on them. Whether or not this was true remains a topic of debate.

6. The famous refrain "Four Dead in Ohio" appears in the protest song "*Ohio*" written by Neil Young and recorded by the group Crosby, Stills, Nash & Young on May 21, 1970 – just 17 days after the shootings at Kent State.

7. The United States eventually withdraw their forces in 1973, but the war continued on and was won by North Vietnam in 1975, thus consolidating the North and the South into the present-day country of Vietnam.

8. J.K. Stoner, "Riot Control Doctrine," *Military Review*, **45** *(2)* 40-44, 1965.

9. In real life, such direct-action campaigns were carried out by the Canadian and Hawaiian Greenpeace organizations between 1975 and 1977.

10. 'Zodiac' is a famous brand of small, rigid-hulled inflatable boats (RIBs) that are prized for their seaworthiness, speed (30 knots or more), and manoeuverability. Although there are other brands, the term Zodiac is frequently colloquially applied to any RIB.

11. Years later, protests such as this would be considered to be part of the 'second-wave of feminism.' Demonstrations and related activities in this period, spanning the 1960s - 1980s, focused on women's cultural and political inequalities in

society.

12. In March 1978, women workers at Fleck Manufacturing went on strike to protest against poor working conditions. They also challenged the (male-dominated) labour movement to support them. The strike was organized and led by women, but it gained the support of the United Auto Workers Union (now Unifor) and the feminist group, Organized Working Women. Eventually, following a bitter strike that shut the plant down and generated national-level media coverage, a settlement was reached with the company. Thereafter, the UAW began to bargain generally for women's issues such as maternity leave, harassment protection, and affirmative action. After numerous bitter strikes at other companies, the Ontario government finally made landmark changes to Ontario labour law. See: M. Landsberg, "Fleck Women Put Fire Back into Feminism," *Toronto Star*, 16 May 1978.

13. Potassium chlorate is a strong oxidizing agent and sugar is very easy to oxidize. When they are exposed to concentrated sulphuric acid, there is an immediate, vigorous reaction that produces heat, purple-tinted flame, and smoke.

14. See *An Inconvenient Mountie* (ISBN: 978-1-9994940-0-1).

15. At this point in time, it was still part of the RCMP Years later, in 1984, the Security Service was spun-out to create the present-day Canadian Security Intelligence Service (C.S.I.S.).

16. See *An Inconspicuous Mountie* (ISBN: 978-1-9994940-2-5).

17. See *An International Mountie* (ISBN: 978-1-9994940-6-3).

18. See *An Indispensable Mountie* (ISBN: 978-1-7772424-2-8).

19. See *An Indestructible Mountie* (ISBN: 978-1-9994940-4-9).

20. See *An Inseparable Mountie* (ISBN: 978-1-7772424-0-4).

21. See *An Inexorable Mountie* (ISBN: 978-1-7772424-4-2).

22. Ottawa's professional football team. At the time, the Ottawa Rough Riders was still in its heyday as a dominant force in the Canadian Football League. It lost its momentum in the 1980s, however, and was wound-up in the 1990s. Ottawa's modern

replacement, the Redblacks, was launched in 2014.

23. Formerly Ottawa's central train station, until the 1960s, this building was the Government Conference Centre, until being turned into a temporary home for Canada's Senate in 2018.

24. The most common type of tear gas is a cyanocarbon called o-chlorobenzylidene, or "CS gas." It isn't actually a gas but is deployed as an aerosol. The CS agent causes tearing and a burning sensation in the eyes, and burning irritation in the nose, mouth and throat. The results are that an affected person has to close their eyes, experiences coughing and difficulty breathing, and becomes disoriented. It has been available since the 1960s.

25. On May 4, 1970, 13 unarmed students were shot by the Ohio National Guard during a peace rally at Kent State University. Four days later, 11 people were bayonetted by the New Mexico National Guard at a University of New Mexico rally. On May 14, two students were killed and many more were wounded by police at a Jackson State University rally.

26. See *An Inexorable Mountie* (ISBN: 978-1-7772424-4-2).

27. See D. Barry, *Icy Battleground. Canada, the International Fund for Animal Welfare, and the Seal Hunt*, Breakwater Books: St. John's, NL, 2005.

28. S. Deyglun, *Les Grands Phoques de la Banquise (The Great Ice Seals)* aired on CBC French, on 17 May 1964.

29. The name International Alliance for Animal Protection and its acronym, IAAP, are entirely fictitious, and are used here as such.

30. Ronald, K. (Chair), "Interim Report to the Minister of Environment from the Committee on Seals and Sealing," 18 January 1972.

31. See *Paris Match*, Issue 1453, 1 April 1977 (cover).

32. The Canadian Police Information Centre (CPIC) is a central police database maintained by the RCMP at its 'HQ' Division in Ottawa. It was launched in 1972 and contains investigative,

identification, intelligence, and ancillary databases which are made available to law enforcement organizations across Canada. Some, but not all, information is also shared with the U.S. National Crime Information Center.

33. 'STEW phone' is reference to a secure telephone capable of providing secure voice communication over non-secure analogue telephone networks. In this case, it was a reference to the STU-I secure telephone unit which was developed in the 1970s by the U.S. National Security Agency. Special variants were provided to selected allies, including Canada.

34. Missing in action (MIA) and presumed dead.

35. *Modus operandi* (MO), meaning a person's method of operation.

36. *The Beachcombers* was a very popular CBC Television series that was originally broadcast from 1972 through 1990.

37. *Charlie's Angels* was an ABC television, crime-drama series that was originally broadcast from 1976 through 1981.

38. The real demonstration calling for a halt to the construction of Ontario's Darlington nuclear generating station was held on 2 June 1979, almost a year later than I have placed in in this story. See D. Fairey, "Nuclear Protesters Invade Hydro Site," *The Canadian Statesman*, Bowmanville, ON, 6 June 1979, pp. 1-2, and S1-S2.

39. In 1978, GLBTQ referred to gay, lesbian, bisexual, transgender, and queer/questioning people. A more current acronym would be LGBTQ+, referring to lesbian, gay, bisexual, transgender, questioning and 'plus,' to represent other sexual identities such as pansexual, asexual, and omnisexual.

40. In the case of the real-life demonstrations, the New South Wales government eventually made legislative changes. In May 1979, the Summary Offences Act was repealed. It had been under the authority of this act that the police had been able to intervene in the demonstrations. Later, in 1984, homosexuality was decriminalized.

41. A somewhat similar series of incidents actually happened in

1979, except that it was the conservation ship *Sea Shepherd* that caught up with the pirate whaler *Sierra* off the Portugese coast. The *Sea Shepherd* rammed the *Sierra,* causing serious damage. Later, when repairs to the *Sierra* were nearly complete, unknown saboteurs used magnetic limpet mines to sink her in Lisbon's harbor.

42. Paraphrased from actual letters written by citizen-opponents of the northwest-Arctic seal hunt. See R. Joyce, "More than One Way to Skin a Seal Hunt," *Maclean's Magazine,* **95** (*12*) 1982, pp. 93-94.

43. This was actually tried in 1983, when the *Sea Shepherd II* blockaded the harbor for two weeks.

44. CP Air (formerly Canadian Pacific Air Lines) flew until 1987, at which time it was bought by Pacific Western Airlines and then absorbed into Canadian Airlines International.

45. Sport utility vehicle.

46. Most of the building remains standing but it's no longer a hotel. In 2013 Memorial University purchased the landmark Battery Hotel and renovated it into a multi-purpose facility that includes a conference centre and graduate student housing.

47. You can't do that walk any more. Many years later (after '9/11' 2001), the city fenced off the best parts of the harbour-walk to provide secure moorage for cruise- and other commercial ships.

48. The expression 'come-from-away' (or 'from away') refers to people that were born outside of Atlantic Canada, and is sometimes used to refer to people born outside of a specific Atlantic Canadian province.

49. An expression meaning 'It's hard to fool a person that's older and wiser.'

50. As it turned out not much actually happened until 1992, by which time the cod stock had dwindled to about 1% of its previous levels. This led to the government declaring a moratorium on the Northern Cod fishery.

51. An expression meaning 'Good luck on your way.'

52. In real life, the 90-foot, 44-gross ton schooner *Scademia* wasn't yet operating in 1979. It was actually built in 1981, and was used for boat tours in and out of the St. John's harbour between 1986 and 2006.

53. Screech is brand of rum originating in Newfoundland and Labrador. Originally a Demerara rum from Guyana, it is now made in Jamaica. At one time, trading ships would take salt-cod south to the Caribbean and bring back barrels of Screech.

54. A classic style of lobster-fishing boat, commonly seen in the Atlantic Provinces. It has a distinctively high bow, from which the gunwales curve down towards a low, flat deck at the stern. Cape Islanders have a reputation for being stable in rough seas.

55. The Witless Bay Seabird Sanctuary comprises four islands in close proximity: Gull Island, Green Island, Great Island, and Pee Pee Island. They were designated as a Wildlife Reserve in 1964, and then re-established under new legislation as a Seabird Ecological Reserve in 1983.

56. This is actually the last line of John Milton's poem "On His Blindness," published in 1673.

57. Sometimes known as a diver's toque, the bright red or reddish-orange knitted-cap was originally a trademark of commercial divers, who wore them under their large brass helmets in the 1800s and early 1900s. When SCUBA diving was brought into broad, non-commercial use by Jacques Yves Cousteau, and others, he and his crew members were often photographed wearing the same bright red toques. As a result, many sport divers picked up the habit as well.

58. An INTERPOL Red Notice is a request to law enforcement worldwide to locate and provisionally arrest a person pending extradition, surrender, or similar legal action.

59. In Canada, most of the Grumman S-2 Trackers were operated by the navy, and were gradually phased out between 1978 and 1990. Many of them, however, were repurposed as Conair Firecat fire-fighting aircraft, in which a large (3,296 litre) fire-

retardant-tank was positioned in the torpedo bay. This allowed them to live on through the early 2000s.

60. See *An Indispensable Mountie* (ISBN: 978-1-7772424-2-8).

61. The *CCGS John A. Macdonald* was classified as a heavy icebreaker, and was named for Canada's first Prime Minister. She was originally commissioned in 1960, as a Department of Transport ship, transferred to the Coast Guard in 1962, and served until 1991, at which time it was decommissioned.

62. The police confrontation with seal-hunt protesters in this story was inspired by a somewhat similar, real-life-incident that occurred in March 1983. The protest-ship *Sea Shepherd II* first blockaded the St. John's harbor, delaying the departure of the sealing fleet by two weeks, then moved into the Gulf of St. Lawrence where it forced several sealing ships away from the harp seal nursery. Two Coast Guard icebreakers carrying 15 RCMP officers blocked and boarded the *Sea Shepherd II*, arresting the captain and 19 crewmembers, all of whom were charged with conspiracy to violate the Seal Protection Act (approaching within a half-mile of a seal hunt and interfering with seal-killing). One of the Coast Guard ships was the *CCGS John A. Macdonald.* See: "Our History," Sea Shepherd Conservation Society, Alexandria, VA, 2017, https://seashepherd.org/our-history/

63. The Messerschmitt-Bölkow-Blohm Bo 105 is a fairly light, twin-engine helicopter. It was introduced into service in 1970. The Canadian Coast Guard Bo 105s were all retired in 2016, but others remain in service in many other countries around the world.

64. Non-Commissioned Officer.

ADVENTURES OF THE FIRST WOMAN MOUNTIE

Book 1: *An Inconvenient Mountie*
Book 2: *An Inconspicuous Mountie*
Book 3: *An Indestructible Mountie*
Book 4: *An International Mountie*
Book 5: *An Inseparable Mountie*
Book 6: *An Indispensable Mountie*
Book 7: *An Inexorable Mountie*
Book 8: *An Intrepid Mountie*
Book 9: *An Intimate Mountie*

www.laurieschramm.ca

www.facebook.com/LaurieSchrammBooks

Laurie Schramm